SPARK OF OPAL

BY MAVIS THORPE CLARK

THE MIN-MIN
IRON MOUNTAIN
SPARK OF OPAL

SPARK OF OPAL

Mavis Thorpe Clark

THE MACMILLAN COMPANY

New York, New York

First published in 1968 by Lansdowne Press, Melbourne, Australia

All characters in this book are fictitious.

Copyright © 1973 Mavis Thorpe Clark
The Macmillan Company, 866 Third Avenue, New York, N.Y. 10022
Collier-Macmillan Canada Ltd., Toronto, Ontario.
Library of Congress catalog card number: 72-81054
Printed in the United States of America

1   2   3   4   5   6   7   8   9   10

Library of Congress Cataloging in Publication Data

Clark, Mavis Thorpe.
  Spark of opal.

  SUMMARY: Discouraged that their family has not made its fortune in the
Australian opal fields, a teen-age brother and sister make a dangerous final at-
tempt to change the family's luck.
  [1. Australia—Fiction. 2. Opals—Fiction]
I. Title.
PZ7.C5495Sp4   [Fic]   72-81054   ISBN 0-02-718950-3

Contents

SPARK OF OPAL

1

Opal Town

It was late mail-day. Inside the Miners' Store, the post office shutter did not go up until five o'clock in the afternoon.

Liz stood first in line with the score or so of bearded men waiting in the corner of this sprawling store. It was a store where men gathered, and it smelled of kerosene and garlic and the strong rubber of the new tires displayed in a rack along the wall. Liz was the only female present.

She listened to the different tongues—Greek, Italian, Yugoslav—with a couple of Australian voices among them. Liz knew the Australians and most of the others, many of whom had permanent dugouts. But the three or four Greeks immediately behind her were strangers, newcomers to the field.

She wondered idly about them and judged, by the way they stood close to each other talking only among themselves, that they knew little English. They were youngish men and might have left their troubled country for political reasons, because of family feuds or simply in the hope of digging a fortune out of the desert.

This Opal Town, one of the few remaining frontier towns in the world, drew the adventurous from all over. They were of many races with Australians, surprisingly, in the minority.

Most of the men were clad only in shorts and thong sandals, with some kind of hat or cap on their heads; one or two wore shirts, in dark colors, undone and floating free. The Australians wore Army-type boots and woolen socks. The dry heat had tanned them all golden-brown rather than black, and the hard work had developed their muscles so that they were all square-shouldered, powerful-looking men. Some smelled of this labor, but Liz did not turn away. Water cost sixty cents for forty gallons.

Now and again a galah with its wing clipped waddled between the many feet and pecked at the straps of her thongs. Sometimes it missed and caught her toe.

Across the wide stretch of concrete floor, on the far wall behind the counter, was a refrigerated food cabinet run by an engine that throbbed continually outside. Every kind of salami, black pudding, liverwurst and cheese could be seen lying colorful, cool and tempting under the scratched glass. Fresh supplies were flown in regularly.

These exotic-looking sausages had come with the increase on the field of men who were not Australians. Liz, nearly sixteen, was old enough to have watched them come and to have noted the changes they brought. Even her own parents ate kabanos now. She liked it herself and was glad she had this sophisticated taste. This sort of thing came from the cities. And at the end of the year she and her father, mother and thirteen-year-old brother Bill would be leaving for Adelaide—that is, if Grandma Birch would give them a home.

The letter she was waiting for now should give the answer to this query, but Liz didn't doubt that it would be yes. Her maternal grandmother would welcome this end to the "gadding," as she called it, of her daughter and her family. She had been trying to bring it about for years.

Liz turned quickly when the young Italian wife of the storekeeper swung open the shutter above the narrow post office shelf on the tick of five o'clock. Her baby, a black-eyed doll, rode on her hip, but she still handled the letters dexterously. She was one of the few women in this town of men, and only a few years older than Liz. Because of this Liz always warmed to her smile, her chatter about her baby and her boyish haircut.

With the shutter open, the Greeks moved up close behind Liz, looking impatient for their mail.

The young woman said, "Won't be long before you leave here, Liz."

"No—just before Christmas."

"After eight years, eh? A long time."

"Yes."

"And no big luck—ever?"

"No."

"It's a shame you go without having found your fortune. Everyone who dig as long—and work as hard—as your father should leave with fortune."

"Dad hasn't given up hope," Liz said. "He refuses to believe he'll leave this place empty-handed. He's certain he'll find a parcel before Christmas. Got a hunch, he reckons."

"Well, he won't be the first who's had such a hunch—a lucky one." The young woman smiled. "Now—only one letter for you, Liz."

As she turned away, Liz felt the eyes of the Greek strangers follow her to the door. She knew she shouldn't have said anything about her father's hunch. It wasn't the sort of thing you talked about on the field. Opal was so unpredictable that many men were guided by such nebulous things as dreams, as a "feel," as a hunch.

She felt a flatness in her stomach as she moved down the line. Surely only the thought of impending departure could have made her so careless. Then she remembered with relief that these newcomers were most unlikely to understand what the word "hunch" meant.

She pushed quickly through the swing door of the store, leaving behind the dim coolness of the high insulated iron roof, the tangled row of miners' carbide lamps hanging from a rafter, the casual display, under glass at one end of the counter, of polished and mounted opal and the glimpse of the green baize of the billiard table in the far annex, partly obscured by a rack of women's cotton dresses.

Liz was wearing a cotton shift. Her bare arms and legs, like those of the men, were smooth golden-brown, and the natural olive tint of her face had the same golden look. Her flaxen hair was straight, and her eyes were as deep a blue as this inland sky. She was below medium height, with a small round figure, but she walked erect and her step was firm.

Her mother often said proudly, "She's the image of my old German grandpa. As German-looking as he ever was."

But except for this German great-grandfather who had once grown grapes in the Barossa Valley, Liz was not German even though she had been christened Ilse. Her father, Mike Watson, would have none of the name and she had grown up as Liz.

Outside the colors were sharp: white-painted store, red stony-dust, a dyed-blue sky, but no green, not even as far as the sharp circle of the horizon.

Liz stepped onto the wide gravel thoroughfare leading down the short slope from plateau to flat. She had to watch out for vehicles swooping in from a maze of rocky off-shoots to this highway—cars, utes, trucks, all old and noisy. The climate and stones, which cut the tires and thumped on sump and undercarriage, aged vehicles quickly here.

Just beyond the Miners' Store was a newly arrived tourist coach. Snub-nosed, it was like an enormous yellow grub with red stripes on its sides. Its passengers would rest overnight at the new motel—built at ground level and kept cool with an air-conditioning plant—and in the morning it would push on for another fifteen hundred miles north.

Meanwhile, passengers were alighting eagerly. The Opal Town! They would write home about the dust, the opal they had bought and the Aborigines they had seen sitting in the shade of the galvanized iron community hall.

Liz paused, too, but not to look at the Aborigines. They were always there in the afternoon shade—twenty or more adults, small dirty black children with tiny desert flies feeding in the corners of their eyes, and babies sitting in the dust or riding on their mothers' backs, tied there with gray blankets. And dogs—as many dogs as Aborigines. They were silent dogs, though sometimes they snarled among themselves and made fierce and lightning attacks on each other, but they were as unmoved by sightseers as were their human companions.

Liz was looking at the tourists. It was September school holidays, and there were a number of young people among them, including several girls her own age. They were all

wearing form-tight slacks in black or pink or blue, and
some had lacy-knit jumpers.

She tried to listen to their casual chatter. But after their
eyes had taken their fill of the dogs and people in the dust,
they turned away and walked down the slope, watching
where they stepped. They had evidently heard that sometimes a piece of opal was to be found among the stones.
Liz smiled then. Opal was hard enough to find at seventy
feet down.

The dark people watched them go, jabbered in their
own Pitjantjatjara tongue and laughed among themselves,
while the dogs sniffed in and out among their legs and the
babies moved about within the confines of the shade and
the group.

It was then that Liz turned and saw Margaret squatting
in the middle of the group, her hair uncombed and dusty,
the whites of her black eyes bloodshot, with little Ruthie
balancing on unsteady feet and clutching at her mother's
shoulder to remain upright.

Margaret was the elder sister of Liz's friend, Kathy.

Margaret, Ruthie and Kathy. These were not Aboriginal
names, and Liz had never heard their Aboriginal names.
Perhaps this generation didn't have any. Liz knew that in
the first years of settlement the Aborigines had not will-
ingly told their tribal names to the white people, because
there were times in a tribal Aborigine's life when it was
taboo for his name to be spoken. So the settlers had given
them European names.

Now, looking at Margaret, Liz couldn't imagine Kathy
ever sitting in the dust like this, with babies clinging to
her, her long eyelashes matted with dust and her hair tangled, with nothing to do but watch the coaches come and
go and be photographed as local color.

The thought caught at her. Why did she imagine that Kathy would not be one of this group one day? Why did she keep telling herself that life would—*must*—offer something different for her friend, when she knew—unless this letter surprised her—that there would be nothing different?

But while she was sure of one affirmative in Grandma Birch's letter, she was almost as sure that there would be one negative.

She went rather moodily down the slope, the pliable soles of her thongs taking the edge off the stones. She didn't often walk, except to and from school. Nobody walked on the field—the dust and the stones were too rough. But her mother had been eager for this letter, and as the old car her mother used had stripped gears and her father had not yet returned from work at the mine, she had walked to the post office.

She wondered if it was a good sign that her father was late. The men seldom worked long into the afternoon if they were not on good trace. How much easier it would be if he struck something good before Christmas! He didn't really want to leave the field, nor did Bill.

Bill was very angry about the move—angry with her. He did not know why she couldn't get a job helping in the store, or even in the post office. Either place would give her a job as she was the only girl of her age in the town. Or she could learn to cut and polish the opal—and be useful in the family when they found a "parcel." He didn't know why she was stupid enough to want to be a teacher—you wouldn't catch him teaching kids! Because of her they had to leave the opal field and go to the city.

Suddenly Liz wished that she was not nearly sixteen, that the time had not yet come when—for her and because of her—they had to leave here. Of course, she had said she could go alone to live with Grandma Birch, that there was no need for them all to go. But her mother would not agree.

"We're sticking together, Liz. Time enough to break up the family when you and Bill marry."

Liz was content with this. She didn't really want to go to town without her mother, even to Grandma Birch's.

She continued down the hill in the wake of the tourists, noting that most of the girls had their hair back-combed into high shapes. Her hand went to her own flat yellow head. Perhaps she would back-comb hers in the city and stiffen it with hair spray; and she thought, "Next year, I'll look just like they do—I'll be part of town."

Somehow, the thought made her feel guilty.

The sun was sinking when she turned west, and above her the now faded blue was shot through with rose, like taffeta, though on the stark black line of the horizon the rose had deepened to vermilion and the sun was a flaming ball that balanced briefly on the sharp edge.

On the flat lay the unmoving dust clouds raised by the miners' vehicles returning home from mines up to twenty miles or more across the desert. The flat was like an inland sea with the dust clouds forming sandbanks and the abandoned derelict cars, their faded colors shining in the oblique rays of the sun, like scattered fishing boats.

As she drew near the top of a low rise, Liz heard the sudden baying of many dogs. She knew the sound. It happened every now and again. Probably one of the pack had displeased and the rest were after it in full cry; or perhaps a feral cat had shown itself and they were in ecstatic pursuit

while the tormented animal scurried ahead, bemoaning
the lack of tree or fence in this woodless land and glad to
find safety at length on top of some forty-gallon oil drum.

Liz topped the rise and saw at once that it wasn't a cat
they were after, but another dog. The hunted was a long
lean animal that barely disturbed a gibber as it skimmed
the ground. The hunters were dogs of all breeds and all
sizes, with long legs and short legs. Both hunted and hunters were rounding the base of the rise. The kangaroo-dog
was already well ahead of his pursuers, and determined to
stay ahead. Liz recognized him at once. Potch! Bill's
Potch.

She couldn't help laughing. Surely no dog in all the
world had been chased so often by his own kind as Potch!
He only had to stray a dozen yards from Bill's heels for the
packs to go after him. It was their sport. Poor Potch. With
ears laid back and long thin tail, curled at the end, acting
as a steering aid, he was heading, without doubt, to where
he believed Bill would be.

And now Bill appeared, accompanied by Steve and
Nikos—Steve who was tall and Aboriginal and Nikos who
was short and Greek.

It was one of the days when Bill was on foot, because
the bicycle he had bought with opal patiently noodled
from the dumps was having its ever-recurring tire trouble.
This was due partly to the sharp stones but also to the
spikes of the bindy-eye seed which were strong enough and
sharp enough to puncture both tire and tube. Until Bill
saved enough for a new tire, his bicycle was out of commission.

Because it was Potch who was being hunted, Bill was
running hard, even faster than Steve, who was like an emu.

And Nikos was running, too, but tailing a bad third on his shorter, heavier legs. The three boys had spread out to confront the pack and were shouting and waving their arms.

Potch, unable to pull up, shot past his master, and Bill slackened enough then to bend as though he were going to pick up a stone.

It was enough. The dogs knew the movement and the accuracy of humans who threw stones. They braked and twisted and cannoned into each other with a quick baring of fangs. Within seconds they were again a silent and businesslike pack, heading hopefully, no doubt, for the waste water pipe at the second store, called the Opal Town Store.

There was no other surface water as far as the pack could travel. Not that the store let much go. They used water as frugally as everyone else, but they didn't have time to cultivate a few plants in pots, and so the packs benefited. There were a hundred such dogs, depending on man to give them a drink because nature withheld water in this desert country.

Now, as his pursuers turned, Potch, tongue lolling, sought the safety of his master's heels. Liz couldn't help laughing.

"That's one thing he can do—run!" she shouted. "You needn't worry—they'll never catch him!"

Bill stroked his dog's head while his two mates indicated their scorn of her laughter by also ignoring her. They knew how Bill felt about Potch and the possibility of having to leave him behind to fend for himself in the Opal Town.

Bill had found Potch on the flat. He was a puppy then, and his left front foreleg was broken—probably the result of a well-aimed stone. He didn't belong to anyone, and how he had managed to keep alive this long was a puzzle. His only hope of food was to follow the pack at a safe distance and gulp down any scraps they missed from the refuse thrown out by the two stores and the motel, native game in the area having been almost wiped out by the gun. But because he was disabled, and because the other dogs bit him when hunger overcame caution and drove him to edge in while they were eating, he was already terrified. Only that hunger, and lonely puppyhood, kept him trailing the pack.

Bill had taken him home and his father, who had a way with all animals, had set his leg. His mother had grumbled about the dog at first, especially as they already possessed an Australian terrier, Nancy, but after a while Potch was allowed freely into the dugout.

He became cheeky enough with humans and would stand up to an adult if he thought any of the family was being molested, but Nancy bossed him and he never lost his fear of his own kind.

Now, after that one gibe, Liz controlled her laughter. She didn't want to make Bill more antagonistic than he was.

As she turned right, skirting the next low round hill toward their dugout, she waved Grandma Birch's letter at her brother, knowing that the sight of it would bring him home as soon as she was.

The three boys followed her at some distance, close together now, their heads down as they talked about things she would not understand. Past fifteen, she was too old for their confidences, and they resented her age.

Watson's Hill—named after their father because he had

been the first to excavate a dugout there—stood a little away from the rest of the low hills that clustered at the base of the plateau. It was somewhat taller, too, and the climb up the wheel tracks to the platform was sharp.

The whitish mullock from their dugout had been leveled to form this raised platform in front of their door into the sandstone hill. At one side was a small galvanized-iron shed, housing their mother's washing machine, and with a shower hose connected to a four-gallon tin on the roof which could be relied on to supply a warm shower at midday. There were more yellow oil drums at the far side, well away from the diesel engine that was placed at the outer edge for safety's sake. The faded blue Holden with its stripped gears was parked close to the rising hillside, and their father's utility now stood outside the fly-wire door.

A pumpkin vine climbed over a bit of wire around the door. It might never bear pumpkins but it was green while it lasted. Their mother fed it with waste water even from the teapot and encouraged it by keeping the large leaves dusted.

Bill and Potch were right behind Liz now. Steve had continued on to the dugout next door where he lived with Carl, their father's partner, and Nikos had hurried on to where, a quarter of a mile distant, he too would disappear into a hill.

From the corner of her eye, Liz saw his short legs running again. He would be in strife with Pappa Melikos tonight, for he was late. Pappa Melikos ruled with a Greek father's ancient right and might. Nikos often complained about it, even to her, and she sometimes had wondered of late why Pappa Melikos permitted this developing friendship with Bill.

2

After Eight Years

THE tunnel into the dugout through the solid sandstone rock was not more than six feet long and led directly into the square-cut living room. There was no door dividing tunnel and room, but when a driving fog of red dust was swirling outside, a curtain was pulled across. In one corner a fire stove was built into the rock, with a flue going straight up through the solid overlay. But since the coming of portagas for cooking, it was used only to warm the dugout in winter. The stone floor had been smoothed with cement and covered with a red linoleum which was kept highly polished. The walls had been adzed to an even surface, but the gypsum specks in the sandstone gleamed like tinsel in the electric light. From outside came the rhythmic throb of the diesel engine that supplied the power.

The Watson family was gathered in the living room—Mike, his wife May, Liz, Bill and the two dogs, Potch and Nancy.

Potch's fawn-gray body was stretched out at Bill's feet,

13

but his head was erect and his ears pricked. He was restless from the tension in the human voices. Nancy slept in a corner of the couch but opened one eye occasionally to note what Potch was doing. He wasn't allowed on the couch.

The family had had their evening meal and the letter had been read in which Grandma Birch had said they could live with her as long as they chose.

"I knew the letter would put the lid on it!" Bill was sharp. "I've seen it coming for weeks—Mum and Liz whispering in corners and having powwows over the dishes."

He was sitting hard back on one of the chairs of the worn lounge suite, each piece of which was pushed square against the wall to save room. One leg was crossed over the other, and the foot in midair was flicking up and down like the tail of an angry cat.

"You don't want to leave, Dad, do you?" he demanded. "It's the women pushing you, isn't it—honestly?"

Mike, stretched comfortably over the other chair, had to be honest when searched by such eager eyes, more green than blue because Bill favored his father's Irish ancestry. "No—I don't want to go. I could go on digging for opal until I died—always believing that some day I'd find the perfect stone."

"And that's what you would do—die—while you were still looking," May snapped.

"Could be a worse death." Mike grinned.

Bill stood up on springy feet, square-shouldered and slim, with promise of being taller than his father. His eyes accused his mother and sister. "There you are—he doesn't want to go! You're pushing him. All because Liz likes reading—an' people say she's clever and ought to be a teacher."

"It isn't just that—and you know it," May said, looking up from the hand-sewing on Liz's new cotton dress. May was not of large build, but sturdy, and she wore her dark straight hair parted at the side and cut in an outdated bob, with a bobby pin to keep the long ends from falling over her face.

Bill went on. "You wouldn't have thought of leaving if Liz hadn't got the idea that she must finish high school and go to the Teachers' Training College!"

Liz said nothing. She knew her good school reports and her teachers' praise pricked her young brother, who was more interested in opal than lessons.

"Your father's not getting any younger—nor me," May pointed out.

"I'm only forty-four," Mike put in mildly.

"Yes—you're only forty-four. You could be good for another ten years here—but then what? Suppose you don't strike any more opal than you've struck in the last eight—what then?"

"Those eight years haven't been that bad, May," her husband protested. "I've earned much more here than I could have earned in the city as a laborer—which is all I was. And I've been my own boss—that's important to a bloke like me."

"I know it's important to you. But we haven't got anything for our old age—and that's important, too. In ten years' time you'll be too old to make a fresh start somewhere else—or at some other job. It has to be now."

"I'm still only a laborer—there won't be any fancy jobs for me back in town," Mike reminded her quietly.

"I know. But *this* job is a young man's job."

"You're dead right," Mike agreed. He stood up and moved into the kitchen which was an excavation on the left of the living room. He was of medium height and light build, but his legs beneath his khaki shorts were muscular, as were his arms revealed by the clean white cotton singlet which May handed to him every night. In this he was different from many of the opal diggers who, without women around, spared neither time nor water for clean singlets.

He took a cup from a shelf fixed to the stone wall, turned the tap half on over the stainless steel sink and watched the water flow quietly into the cup. It never ceased to amaze him that in his dugout he now had a tap from which water flowed.

Certainly the supply was limited, coming by gravity flow from the two-thousand-gallon tank higher up the slope. They had had the tank only since the desalination plant and bore, which brought saline water up from nearly three hundred feet and desalted it with the heat from the sun, had been installed. Now it was possible to get the tank filled in the summer when the plant was working at its peak under a sun temperature of 140° and the population of the Opal Town was at its lowest ebb.

He half-filled the cup, then carefully withdrew his upper set of false teeth and dropped them in. He didn't like those teeth. He'd had them a year and worn them less than half of that time, and never while working in the mine. But May said when they got to town he would not be able to go without them; it put you into a low kind of social set if you didn't wear teeth in the city. A depressing thought.

"I can't understand you two!" Bill was biting. "You've always told Liz and me how you loved adventure, that that was what brought you to the opal fields in the first place."

Mike sprawled again in the chair. "It's a true tale," he said dreamily. "I was restless as a flea when the war finished and I came back from Malaya. Tried different jobs in different parts of the country. Then I met your mother—and she liked moving around, too." He grinned at her, with no top teeth. "It's just eight years since we tossed that coin—to the cane cutting in Queensland or to opal mining on this opal field. And the opals won."

"But *we* haven't!" snapped May.

Mike's grin became a frown. "We lived in a tent on the flat when we arrived here first. We burned through the summer and we shivered through the winter. And regularly the tent blew down around us. Remember? Now, you've got a stainless-steel sink, a portagas stove, a washing machine, a refrigerator and a comfortable home—even if it is carved out of a hill."

"But I haven't *got* anything—like money in the bank."

"You've got this . . ." Mike went to the drawer in the blackwood sideboard—bought secondhand in Adelaide, like the rest of their furniture, transported home on the utility three years ago and nearly left on the wayside when they were bogged in sand fifty miles down the track. He pulled out the drawer, put his hand up into a secret cavity he'd made in the drawer slot and drew forth forth a small cardboard box. As he placed it on the Laminex table top they all leaned forward. It didn't matter how many times they looked, the fires always burned differently.

The opal was mounted in a ring, and the fire in it was mostly red but shot through with violet, blue and green. The flames leaped as Mike turned it to the light.

"Three hundred and fifty quid's worth . . ." he murmured. He always said it. It was part of the ritual.

But this time, with school-teaching promising in the future, Liz said, "Seven hundred dollars, Dad—you should start to think in dollars."

"Three hundred and fifty quid," Mike repeated. "Put it on your finger, May; it looks good on your finger."

May slipped the ring onto her third finger, next to the scratched gold wedding ring. She turned it this way and that, the rainbow colors flashing deep and brilliant. Her eyes softened at the beauty of this stone, which had been cut from the solid middle of an opalized mussel shell. Mike had found it in the first shaft he'd ever sunk.

There had been no seam opal in this shaft but nature, using cunning to bind forever this new recruit, had rewarded Mike with a small pocket of shells. Only one of these was a "full" shell of solid opal; the rest were "skin" shells opalized only in thin curved outline and of little value except as specimens. But the one full shell had yielded this single perfect gem.

May had said then, "We'll never sell this stone, Mike— this is *our* stone."

As soon as they could afford to do so, they had had it cut and polished by an expert and set in this fine 18-carat gold setting.

They had not found another stone worth seven hundred dollars. Mike had never struck it rich, but there had been good patches and good times. There were exciting summer holidays to Adelaide and Sydney. They had made enough to excavate and furnish this dugout, to buy a compressor, a lighting plant, a diesel engine and, as their first vehicle wore itself out on the gibbers, to replace it with another— secondhand because a new vehicle was wasted on this type of country—and yet another. The present utility was solid and roomy enough to carry most of their goods back to Adelaide.

But this last year or so had been bad—barely tucker money from shaft after shaft. And constant overhead expenses were high for such things as gelignite—a case or more a week—petrol and maintenance for their vehicles, oil for the compressor. Their savings had ebbed. It was Carl—the Austrian mate whom Mike had taken a couple of years ago—whose money was keeping things going now.

The hard part to bear was that there were some rich finds being made on the field.

May turned her hand to catch the light. It was not a beautiful hand. Her hands had coarsened during those early days in the tent when she had helped on the windlass while Mike, with pick and shovel, had sunk shaft after shaft, some to the seventh level, ninety feet down. "We'll never sell this stone," she vowed dreamily.

"Aw-w . . ." Bill's eyes leaped with the myriad dance of color. "You two make me sick."

"Bill!" His mother was angry. "Don't talk that way! Sometimes I think Dad should be like Pappa Melikos and keep his son in order. The trouble is, we're too easy with you—let you know all our business and have your say in everything."

Bill offered a half-grin of apology. "But, Mum, you know how it is with opal. You have to wait for the bit with your name on it—like your ring. I know there's even a bit with *my* name on it—Old Welhelm reckons so. Couldn't we wait?"

"Time is down to the remainder of this year, Bill. Liz is going to proper high school in the new year."

Mike sat a little straighter then. "I'm hopeful, Carl's

hopeful," he put in mildly. "We're on good trace. But it's leading us a bit of a dance—we badly need a real pointer for the direction of the main run."

"Where is the mine, Dad?" Bill was eager. "You've been pretty cagey about it."

"I've been waiting for you to tell me."

"What d'ye mean?" Bill screwed up his green-blue eyes.

"Thought your pal Nikos would have told you. We've sunk a shaft out at the Greek Patch—just across from Nikos's father."

"At the Greek Patch?" Bill was surprised.

"Yes. Only two or three Aussies out there."

"And Nikos knows?"

"If he doesn't, he goes around with his eyes shut."

"But he hasn't said . . ."

"I gathered that. Reckon his father has told him not to talk opal to you. Same as I'm telling you not to talk opal to him. In fact, I'd rather you didn't talk to him at all."

"But we're mates."

"O.K. But don't give anything away—keep your mouth shut. We'll probably take you out there at the weekend. Hope to need your help—and Steve's also, by then."

At the mention of Steve's name, Bill's brightness switched off like a light.

"You know what you're doing to Steve by going, don't you?" he said fiercely. "Carl's going to throw it in, too, and go back to Austria. His mother's been wanting him to go long enough—and now he reckons there's nothing to stay for. Well, what's going to happen to Steve? He's got used to living with Carl."

"I expect he'll have to go to a Home down in Adelaide," Mike said quietly. "And make no mistake—Carl feels badly about Steve. He'd take him with him, but he knows he wouldn't fit in his country or be happy there. In any case, in a year or so Steve's going to become a police cadet."

Bill stood very straight, eyes tightened. "Why can't we take him to Grandma Birch's place with us?" He looked from father to mother.

It was May who answered. She had been dreading this question, especially as she, herself, would like to have taken over the care of Steve from Carl and knew that Mike felt the same. But the question of a roof over their heads had also to be met.

There was that paragraph, too, in Grandma Birch's letter which she hadn't read out. It said, "You asked me, May, about the two Aborigines, Steve and Kathy—I couldn't have them living with us. They don't know how to live properly, do they? I don't think the neighbors would like it."

May hadn't let even Mike see that paragraph. If he read that, he would live in a tent rather than agree to live with Grandma Birch.

Now she met Bill's question head on. "The house is too small—it's going to be a squeeze to fit ourselves in. And Grandma Birch doesn't like Aborigines."

"Why? What's wrong with them?"

"Nothing. Grandma just doesn't understand—she's always lived in the city and hasn't had anything to do with them."

"Then we could teach her by taking him there."

"He can't go with us, Bill."

"Why can't we get our own house?"

"We haven't enough money."

May pushed the ring toward her daughter. "Put it back in its box, Liz," she said, her voice flat.

Liz slipped the ring onto her finger and turned it about as her mother had done. She didn't even mention Kathy's name. It would do no good, for she realized that Grandma would make no difference for sex. Not that there was any real need to worry about Steve, though Bill was being so noisy. Steve would get along anywhere. He had pride in himself: first from his own father who had fought for Australia in the Second World War, and then from Carl, the Austrian.

Steve was different from Kathy. Kathy was a girl who had roamed the desert and lived now on the flat in a derelict, long-abandoned caravan, and whose sister sat in the dust and shade of the galvanized iron shed.

Some of the depression that had taken hold of Liz in the Miners' Store that afternoon returned. Although she was looking forward to life in the city and the wider scope of education it offered, she began to feel wretched. As soon as possible she must tell Kathy that she was going away; she could delay it no longer. She must give the girl time to get used to the fact.

Perhaps there would be an opportunity tomorrow when the school made the trip to Water-Hole Creek for the annual picnic and swimming sports.

She took off the ring and put it back in its box. It was a beautiful stone, but she didn't tingle to its beauty as her mother did or feel the excitement that it aroused in Bill and her father. She was not obsessed by opal.

Bill suddenly hit the table with his fist. "What about Potch?" he shouted. "I'm not leaving him. If you can take that mong Nancy, I can take Potch."

"There's no room for a big dog in a small yard," May said. "In any case, Grandma doesn't like dogs. She's making a special concession for Nancy because she's small."

"I'm not leaving Potch. I'll make my own plans!"

Mike leaned over and turned up the radio. "Stop your shouting! All sorts of things can happen in three months."

Bill still shouted. "There's one thing that won't be different. We'll be going to town. Mum's made up her mind. She wants Liz to meet kids her own age and go to parties —I've heard them! Aw-w—come on, Potch!"

The dog rose, thin-flanked, pointed nose drooping, ears flat. He stood back until he saw which way the boy was going, then he started to follow down the tunnel to the outer door. Nancy woke up then and, with tail raised importantly, yapped at his heels, putting him out of the dugout. She was the one dog Potch didn't run from, but neither did he retaliate.

Bill's foot shot out and he caught the terrier in the middle. "Little rat!"

"Bill!" cried May.

Bill's face flushed red and he hurriedly swung the door open to a black night sky, sprinkled with the white confetti of stars and divided with the smeary brush mark of the Milky Way. On the earth the only light was the occasional electric light globe at the entrance to a dugout; the only sound was the throb of the invisible diesel engines.

Once beyond the white circle from the globe above the doorway, Bill could not see his own feet, but Potch's warmth was close to him and he touched the dog's head. Looking up, he vowed to the stars, "I'll think up *some* plan!"

3

❖

Water-Hole Creek

It was spring, and in a few places there were signs of the season in the desert. The patchy rain of a month ago had decorated isolated stretches of gibbers with the green of earth-hugging succulents. Here and there, too, were the yellow of cushion-topped billy buttons, the lolly-pink of the open-faced parakeelya, waving stretches of pussy-cat tails and an occasional trail of sturt pea with its bewhiskered scarlet-faced flowers. But these scattered signs of spring served only as a contrast to the burnt red earth and the polished stones where no rain had fallen.

The Land Rovers were traveling at a steady pace along the faintly defined track across the gibber plain, which was not the usual route to the Water-Hole Creek. They had taken this longer route so that they could edge the strange stretch of country that the sea had once washed over—possibly a hundred million years ago. Nothing grew there now, but shells and petrified wood from a long-vanished forest lay exposed on the surface.

The two vehicles, their canvas hoods rolled down, were each crammed with more than twenty children, more dark-skinned ones than white. They sang "Waltzing Matilda" and "Song of Australia"—which they were practicing for the school end-of-the-year break-up—to the accompaniment of the hum of engines and tires, and these were the only sounds in the desert. There were no birds, not even a wedgetailed eagle spiraling into the high blue sky; and, apart from meager saltbush, no tree or shrub was growing. Only this cavalcade broke the quiet and gave movement to the landscape.

This was the country which explorer John McDouall Stuart had wandered over more than a hundred years earlier. Describing his journey, he had written, "It was a rough, terrible trip."

But the children traveling in the Land Rovers were unaware of the land's viciousness. There were picnic baskets under the improvised seats along the sides, and some of the boys were wearing their swimming trunks, ready for the water hole, with towels tied around their necks.

That was why they grumbled when Mr. Peter Robbins, the slightly balding head teacher of their Special Rural School, stopped the vehicles on this dead-looking area of the earth's surface and ordered them to jump out. Mr. Robbins could have had a promotion long ago if, on the death of his wife and with no children of his own, he hadn't accepted these scholars of so many shades of color as his charges. But that didn't mean he didn't get things done *his* way, so the children jumped smartly enough from the vehicles.

Even though it was the day of the picnic and swimming sports, Mr. Robbins saw no reason why he should not impress on them something of this strange land—the oldest continent in the world—in which they lived. Also, it justified the twenty-one-mile journey to the water hole!

The surface here undulated like a slow ocean swell. Stony dust rose up around their ankles—petrified dust that once may have been the mud of a sea bed, although there was no ordinary sea sand here. But between the overlay of gibbers there were tiny black pebbles of ironstone, polished black and smooth by driving winds and thick as confetti. Perhaps long ago a great mountain of ironstone had reared above this vanished sea, or perhaps a petrified crust had formed where the sea had receded and, in turn, had weathered and broken into these stones.

There were other stones, of regular pattern—left in heaps as a tide leaves its debris—that only those children who had been to the seashore recognized as sea-shell shapes. Shapes that were the same as the mussels they had gathered, or the bonnet shells, or the fan-shaped scallop shells, or the rounded cockles. There were stone tree trunks, too, that had been left embedded in the mud of that long-ago tide that had receded and never returned. But these trees, unlike the sea shells, were of no known living species.

Peter Robbins had his two teacher-assistants—Liz, his senior pupil, and Sister Joan Brown, the Sister-in-Charge of the Opal Town's hospital—to help supervise the children. If possible, Sister Joan always arranged with Sister Alice—who comprised the rest of the hospital staff—to have her day off coincide with any excursion such as this, partly because she liked to see the country, but mainly because she was particularly interested in the welfare of the Aboriginal children and never missed an opportunity to be with them.

Sister Joan may have been thirty but today, clad in a short pink cotton dress and sandals, with a smart mop-cap on her dark head, she would have passed for a contemporary of Liz's. She giggled along with the children as she helped gather them around Mr. Robbins while he talked about the tremendous pressures and changing temperatures that had thrust the sea back, sealed the living shellfish forever within their shells and left an aridity that, over those millions of years, had turned the shells, the mud and the trees to stone.

Many of the children had never seen the sea, and though Mr. Robbins had shown them slides of a great stretch of shimmering blue which he said was the ocean, they could not connect these stone shells with water. The stones they knew—of any shape—were part of waterless country.

So they whispered and giggled as their bare feet sank into the grayish dust, until Mr. Robbins raised his voice and silenced them. He was determined that they should know more about these stones than that they had been there since the beginning of the Dreamtime.

Then he allowed each of them to find a specimen for himself—a mussel, a scallop shell, a sea-snail shell, a broken piece of petrified wood. It was Nikos, Bill Watson's friend, who found the perfect fan shell.

Nikos was not one of Mr. Robbins's scholars, his father having sworn—when Nikos joined him earlier in the year —that his son was past the school-leaving age of fifteen. But today, to everyone's surprise, Pappa Melikos had given permission for the boy to join this school outing.

The shell was a great prize. It was complete even down to the tiny "ears" at the base, and Bill wished for a moment that he had found it himself. Any tourist off the

coach would pay a good price for such a beautiful specimen.

But it was a passing envy. Nikos was his friend, and Bill
advised him to stuff the shell carefully into his pocket and
show his father. "Reckon he might let you come to school
when he sees what kind of things we learn about," he said.
"Don't you think so, Mr. Robbins?"

But Mr. Robbins doubted that Nikos's father would let
him come to school. He was too useful on top of the mine,
working the winch, even though Mr. Robbins was sure
that he wasn't a day older than Bill.

Then they piled back into the Land Rovers again to sing
the rest of their way to the Water-Hole Creek.

From five miles off they could see the line of mulga
along the watercourse. The creek bed was at the bottom of
the dropped edge of the tableland, the seventy-foot drop
giving the effect of a split level to the earth's surface.

The wide shallow bed was dry and never carried more
than a flash flood. But the rain of a month ago had filled a
close chain of water holes and because they were deep—
fifteen to twenty feet—water would remain in them, even
without replenishment, for a considerable time.

Those last five miles were slow going, for the vehicles
had to plow through heavy sand, and when at last they arrived, Liz was glad to stretch her legs. As she jumped from
the Land Rover, Kathy followed her. Kathy had been close
to Liz throughout the journey and while on the site of the
ancient sea bed had helped to bunch the younger children,
though they hadn't taken much heed of her because, like
Nikos, she was new to the field—or new, at least, from
early in the year.

Kathy had come to the field with George Murphy's

mob. She was the daughter of a recently deceased brother, which made George Murphy, by tribal law, as responsible for her as if he were her own father. And an Aborigine, even a sophisticated one like George Murphy, never shirked such family responsibilities. The girl had had intermittent schooling at various mission stations and spoke English, as well as her own Antakirinja tongue.

Like Nikos, no one knew exactly how old she was, for her mother had been traveling with the tribe when she was born and no one had noted the year. But Mr. Robbins had taken a guess that she was in her early teens.

Now as Liz moved toward the shade of the mulgas, Kathy moved with her.

Not all the children could swim, and the shallow pools where they might have paddled had long dried out, so swimming was put off until after lunch and a peanut hunt in the sand organized for the interim. Mr. Robbins had brought a small sack of peanuts with him, and while Sister Joan unpacked the picnic baskets he ordered his charges to gather on the far side of the Land Rovers and shut their eyes while he and his assistants hid the peanuts.

Judging by the tightly screwed-up eyes, this order was obeyed, but as soon as he called: "Are you ready?" the children scattered to scuffle in the warm red sand, to turn over rocks and bits of broken mulga wood.

Bill and Steve worked as a team, as they always did, with Nikos as a third but separate partner. Bill and Steve were pooling their finds with the unspoken intention of sharing the prize, but Nikos was a single unit. He was Bill's new friend but hadn't graduated to complete equality.

The three boys were of different height, Steve being the

tallest and at least three inches over Bill. He was very straight, slim of hip, broad of shoulder, and would grow to a big man. His mother had been a full blood but his father half-caste, and his features had the longer European structure. He wore his hair very short and slicked hard down with hair oil. He was scarcely darker skinned or darker eyed than Nikos, the Greek. Nikos was not really fat, but he was of much rounder build than either of the other two and moved with a slight roll.

Liz watched them quietly for a time, then began lazily to turn over the sand or a bit of wood with her foot. That was when Kathy began to go, with unerring accuracy, to this spot and that—always returning with a handful of peanuts.

"But Kathy, how do you know just where to look?" cried Liz, stuffing her two pockets and then her handkerchief with the nuts.

"Want you to win," said Kathy, without hesitation.

"But you can win, yourself—keep them."

"No!" Kathy was determined. "Help you to stay."

So that was it! Liz sighed as she followed her friend along the creek bed.

In the schoolyard that morning, while waiting for the arrival of the Land Rovers, Liz had chosen a moment when there had been excited shouting and milling around them to break the news to Kathy that soon she would be leaving the Opal Town.

She would never forget the expression that had dulled Kathy's face. The shininess of eyes and smile had died instantly, and she had stood still. Then the Land Rovers had arrived and she had followed Liz into the vehicle with no spring in her feet, but she had sat very close for the entire trip.

Kathy was taller than Liz and very thin, her bare feet wide and sprawling. Her hair was curly, but not frizzy, and hung loose to her shoulders, while the smear of rust color in the ends reminded Liz of the smear of billy-button yellow on the plain. Her mouth was wide and friendly and her teeth large and strong and white. Every now and again she made a swoop under stone or wood, and as the number of peanuts grew, Liz accused her. "You must have looked . . ."

" 'Course," said the girl. "How else you win—against all of 'em?" She pointed to the hot, scurrying small ones. "An' I want you to stay."

"I have to go—the whole family has to go."

"Where will *I* go?" demanded Kathy. "Where?"

"You've got George Murphy, and all those relations," Liz said. She couldn't shut out the picture of Kathy's home from her mind. That sun-bleached caravan with no glass in the window frames, the campfire in the lee of the bulldozer mullock heap, the family grouped around it, sitting tightly together, shoulder to shoulder, eating their watery oatmeal for breakfast, and the dogs pressing tightly into their backs in the hope of being remembered and fed and given a drink.

Kathy looked down at the large gathering of peanuts in her skirt.

"Give them to the little ones," Liz said kindly. "I'm too big to collect the prize anyway."

Without a word, the dark girl turned and thrust peanuts into the sweaty hands of the small ones, white and dark alike. They swarmed around her, shouting for more, but not once did she smile.

And then Sister Joan called them to their meal. They were each given a sandwich, previously prepared in the school staff room, made of three thick slices of bread, and between each slice as much nourishment as Joan Brown could fit—Vegemite laid on with a heavy hand, a slab of cheese, shredded cabbage, a slice of tinned meat loaf and tomato. For many of the children this was their only good meal of the day.

Liz helped to hand out each package as she did at school.

"I saw what Kathy was up to," Joan told her. "That girl dotes on you, Liz. I was at the school when the group from the Reserve arrived this morning, and she said to me: 'Had two showers at the Reserve this morning, Sister Joan—I'm going to sit next to Liz in the Land Rover.'"

"It is a—kind of—responsibility, Sister Joan," Liz said, wishing silently that she knew just how to handle such a responsibility. It wasn't as though she was used to having girl friends, even white ones. No girls of her own age had grown up with her in the Opal Town, and the few who had come later had been younger. That was why she and her mother were so close. But it didn't make it any easier for her to handle Kathy's tense devotion—born the day the girl had arrived new at school, out of the desert, and Liz had tried to make it easier for her.

"Kathy's one of the Aborigines who could be helped to a better life than noodling for a living around the mine dumps," Joan said. "It's a pity you're going from here— your influence over her might be the thing to save her from becoming part of that group that sits in the dust with the dogs."

Liz made no reply. She couldn't bring herself to tell Sister Joan of Kathy's reaction to her leaving, and was glad when Mr. Robbins announced that all the vitamins must surely be digested and they could swim.

Most of the dark children who had had access to water holes sometime during their walkabouts were able to swim—not in any particular orthodox fashion, but to move their arms and legs with rhythm and keep afloat. Bill could swim, Steve's father having taught him years ago. Before he died, Steve's father had been a stockman on Water-Hole Creek Station. One day he had laughed and pushed the small white boy into a concrete tank at a bore where Steve was already splashing, and said, "Swim out."

Bill, with Steve beside him to show how, had swum or flapped out, and soon he had been able to swim as well as Steve. Now they were teaching Nikos, even though the bottom was twenty feet below him. Nikos spluttered and spat out frothy water, but each time he was about to sink Steve was there to propel him upward.

They tired at length and lay out on the pebbly bank to dry. Liz noticed that Bill and Steve lay a little apart from Nikos, and presently, while Nikos's eyes were closed, they stood up and, with their half-wet towels tied around their necks, began to walk slowly away up the stony creek bed. They walked close together, their heads down and their voices low.

Liz thought she knew what it meant. They were making the plans that Bill had said he would make. For eight years they had planned together. They were mates and no matter how stubborn and cagey Bill might be, Steve would back him; and it would be good backing, for Steve was as smart as Bill and much better at lessons.

Liz just hoped that the plan wouldn't be prickly like a bindy-eye burr.

They were gone half an hour at least and Nikos was beginning to look lonely and miserable as he sat on the bank, watching the swimmers—all younger than himself—enjoying the water hole. He couldn't trust himself to the twenty feet without Steve and Bill to support him. But the next time Liz looked his way he had disappeared.

To Liz's surprise, Bill and Steve returned looking glum, and she couldn't resist asking, "Got a plan yet, Bill?"

He answered savagely, "No! Except that we *have* to find opal."

"Dad is trying . . ." Liz cautiously reminded him.

"We need enough—at least—for a deposit on a house in Adelaide."

"A deposit on a house!" Her young brother never ceased to astonish her. He hated school work but surely was as shrewd as a monkey.

"The thing is—if we have our own house to go to, we can have anyone we want to live with us."

Liz nodded. Yes, their parents would be more than willing to have Kathy and Steve, and Potch as well as Nancy.

"But we haven't come up with any good ideas!" Bill was bitter that two minds, for once, weren't any better than one. "The only thing is—we'll louse the dumps."

Liz frowned. "Noodle sounds better."

"Old-timers, like Old Welhelm, reckon there's plenty of bits of opal still in the mullock. But it's no use telling Dad we want to do this—it'd hurt his pride to know we were lousing the dumps for him."

"It certainly would," Liz said hastily.

"Anyway, last night he said that he and Carl will need us at the weekend. So that leaves only after school. And he and Mum won't like that—they'll say I have to do my homework. But you could help here."

"Me? How?"

"Cover up for us when we're late home. Say we're

staying back after school for extra work. Reckon that's the least you can do."

Liz felt the prod. Then she looked across to where Kathy was sitting alone on a rock with hair dangling, bare toes kicking the dust. She was woebegone. Even a bottle of warmish Coke from the crate donated by the Opal Town Store could not cheer her. She put her head back and sucked slowly and sadly at the bottle opening.

Liz sighed. "All right—I'll do it, though I warn you I'm not much good at story-telling."

"It's not much to ask!" Bill said roughly. "You might get roped in for something really big when we hit on a *real* plan. And we will! Soon!"

Liz found herself hoping then that such a plan wouldn't materialize. Without a doubt, when it came, it would be a proper bindy-eye.

Then they heard Nikos give a shout—almost a shriek. It was from up the creek, beyond the first patch of mulga.

"Ow! Ow-w!" It was as staccato as a pistol shot.

"Ste-eve! Bill-l!"

The two boys tensed, then they turned as one and leaped away. Liz followed and she saw Kathy come to life, too, and head after them.

Nikos was just beyond the first patch of trees. He had gone looking for bits of different-colored jasper to polish in the wind-driven tumbling machine he had made, and was standing now in the middle of the dry creek bed with a toss of rocks, big and small, resting on the gritty bed around him. His black eyes were wide and his fingers pointed unsteadily.

"S-s-snake!"

Bill jumped forward. "Bit you! Where? Let's see it!"

Nikos still spluttered and pointed.

"Where?" Bill was sharp. "Your leg? Your foot? Tell us quick. Give us yer knife, Steve!"

As Steve thrust his hand into the belt at his waist, Nikos managed to say, "No-o—not bit!"

"Well-l!" It was hard to say whether Bill was disappointed or not at being unable to practice bush surgery. "Then what are you yelling for?"

Nikos couldn't believe such nonchalance. "But it was a snake! Crawled over my toes—while I sat here on this rock, looking at my fan shell. I threw the shell at it and it disappeared—under there." He pointed to a small boulder in front of him.

"Aw—what's a snake unless it bites you? You make a heck of a noise."

But Nikos hadn't been brought up with snakes. He had come to Australia as a baby from Kythera, one of the islands of Greece, and lived in a dense Melbourne suburb until his father had brought him to the opal fields early this year. He had grown up to speak Greek and Australian and to envy the freedom of the Australian boys of his age, but he had never had a snake crawl over his feet before.

"It crawled over my toes . . ." he reiterated.

"But it didn't bite 'em—so that's all right," Bill said, bending down. "Here's your shell—but you've busted it. Look—a tiny chip out of the top of the fan."

Nikos took the shell quickly. "It hit that rock," he said, eyeing the flaw with disappointment. Then he brightened. "But I reckon it helped hurry that snake off. The thing might have turned and bitten me if I hadn't thrown the shell at it. Reckon it's my lucky shell."

" 'Course it's lucky," Bill said. "It's a hundred million years old—and you found it."

He was turning away when Kathy dropped on her knees to look at the sand in front of the boulder.

"Mulga snake," she said, her mouth wide in a white-toothed grin. "Not bite—good to eat."

Steve looked down from his superior height. "A brown snake—and dangerous," he said with finality.

"No," Kathy shook her head. "See the squiggles—this way, that way, long one, short one—that one mulga snake."

"Brown snake," Steve said firmly.

"Bet he's right," said Bill. "He knows brown snakes."

Kathy picked up a thin tough bough of mulga and began to dig around the bottom of the boulder. Although she was sure it was a mulga snake, she went about her task warily. Some snakes were deadly, and the women of her tribe were always cautious in their approach to any snake. Excited now, she spoke quickly, in Antakirinja. "Mulga snake—not too big."

She dug dexterously, and soon the snake was on the end of her stick. A writhing brown, yellow-bellied mulga snake. Even if it had no animosity to anyone it looked fearsome enough with head weaving from side to side and tongue darting. Kathy dropped it and killed it almost in one action.

Then she looked up to grin shyly at Steve. She didn't often speak to Steve, for he was older and bigger and growing quickly toward a man. In any case, the white man's boots he wore to school—never thongs—and the red socks intimidated her.

At school he hardly ever spoke to her, and while her mind wandered, he was always intent on the lessons. He seemed to want to learn, while she found it hard to sit still, hard not to stare outside at the hot sun or the red dust-cloud. He was in the top grade, of course, and she was still puzzling over sums in the third class. Sometimes, when the three or four pupils who had reached the exaltation of top grade were doing a science experiment, such as the sublimation of iodine, she watched Steve. Without doubt he found it interesting to see the purple crystals form in the bowl above the flame of the metho-burner and would ask, or answer, questions.

Now she said apologetically, "Mulga snake." Perhaps it would have been better for it to have been a brown snake. A *nyitayira* did not like to be proved wrong by a *kungka*, and she regretted that it had turned out to be a mulga snake.

Steve grinned. "So it is. Reckoned I knew, Kathy—but I didn't. Must be forgetting."

Kathy said in her own Antakirinja, "I dig them—many times."

Steve's mother had been of the Pitjantjatjara tribe, but there were some similarities in the dialects and he remembered enough for him to understand. He said, "O.K., you win."

And then everyone looked at Nikos who was regarding the dead snake with extreme dislike. He just didn't believe that it was harmless, and he could still feel the scales slithering over his feet as he sat on the rock and the deadly fear that for a second had immobilized him. It was the first snake he had seen so close, but he could not admire the brown and yellow markings.

"Sure you're not bit?" Bill eyed the Greek boy with the look of one who could enjoy even delayed surgery.

"Bitten," Liz corrected.

"No." Nikos was sure. He knew what Steve's knife looked like.

Kathy severed the snake's head with a sharp mulga chip then picked up the body again with the long stick.

"I'll take it back to George Murphy," she explained. "He like this snake—good to eat."

"No!" exclaimed Liz. "You can't, Kathy! I'm not having that thing wrapping up my feet in the Land Rover. Leave it here."

Obediently, Kathy dropped the brown and yellow body, and they turned, as a group, back toward the rest of the picnickers.

"Gee . . ." mused Steve to Bill. "Never thought I wouldn't be able to recognize the track of a mulga snake. Not going to be as good as my old man, Bill. He could recognize and follow any track—bird, beast or man."

4

The Stolen
Compressor

THEY spent the whole day at the Water-Hole Creek, and it
was early evening when the two Land Rovers pulled into
the town. The miners had already returned home and
mushroom clouds of red dust hung low over the flat.

It was a very still evening with delicate shades of mauve
and rose in the tall sky directly above. The horizon that
encircled the flat plate of the earth was a black rim, shot
with red where the sun had slipped over.

The two vehicles dropped children along the way, some
being left at the Aborigines' Reserve. The vehicles waited
here, too, while Kathy and the other dark children who
did not live here changed from the school clothes given
out by the Superintendent each morning into their own
ragged clothing. On all school mornings these children,
whose parents did not care for the more restricted life on
the Reserve, were picked up by truck from the scattered
camps and, before being taken to school, were brought
into the Reserve and supervised while they had showers

and changed their clothing. In the afternoon the procedure was reversed.

This evening, after leaving the Reserve, Kathy was next to be dropped from the Land Rover. Jumping down, she started to run quickly over the stones toward the caravan. Liz watched her go and saw that the Murphy family was already having their evening meal.

They were sitting in a circle around a small fire from which thin smoke arose, soft and gray. Two or three naked children were milling around with the dogs, and every now and again a woman lifted a blackened pot from the fire and stirred the contents. Once she went to the water barrel and the dogs followed, pressing close, but she didn't seem to notice. The Aborigines' dogs were always the thirstiest, for water was never plentiful at the camps on the flat.

Kathy didn't look back as she ran lightly, but with little grace, across the gibbers, her long, loose dress flapping. Liz knew that she was sore inside—that it hadn't been a happy day for her. Even knowing that it was a mulga snake and not a brown one hadn't helped her, because she liked to find favor in Steve's eyes.

She was silly to run, Liz thought crossly—to run to that home where there was no kitchen, no tap except on the forty-four-gallon drum that stood beside the caravan, no chairs, no table—nothing at all except a cluster of people, a small fire and what shelter an old car with the tires removed and a windowless caravan could give. Certainly it was only a few years since they had given up using the age-old *gunyah*, or bough shelter, and perhaps their present accommodation made more solid windbreaks. But soon it would be dark and there would be nothing to do but huddle tightly together, dogs as well, and sleep till morning.

The morning would bring school for those of school age. For the rest it would bring noodling for the wherewithal to live, and sitting in the dust.

The Aborigines of this state had recently been made free and equal citizens with the white man, which meant that there were no more handouts and they were expected to earn their own living. Few of them on the opal fields had any trained skills and, in any case, there was no work for them here—or, in fact, for anyone other than the actual opal miner.

So the Aborigines of this area made their living by noodling. It was the women mostly who searched the dumps for the bits of opal that the miners missed. The rubble that was tossed out from a hole was free to be "noodled" or picked over, for the Miners' Right applied only to the treasure found below the surface. With long iron "gin" bars—one end flattened and pointed up with a rock—the women would stir and dislodge the heaped sandstone, their sharp eyes discerning the flash of color that would supply the money for their needs.

But the Aborigines were not attracted to the opal as such. There were well-founded rumors among the whites that it figured in their ritual life, and this, perhaps, explained their reticence and professed ignorance of the stone. But it was found in waterless country where yams did not grow nor game abound. Before the coming of the white man, this had been considered "not-good" country, to be avoided. Nor were the Aborigines—the full-bloods, anyway—attracted to those deep narrow holes going down into cold darkness that was as fraught with evil as night shadows were.

However, the dumps at least offered a source of income

that could be garnered while the sun shone. In the light of morning, Liz knew, Kathy's relations—her sister Margaret and her aunt and her aunt's children—would take their iron bars and go in search of bits of opal.

After Kathy, Nikos was next to be dropped from the Land Rover, his stone fan-shaped shell still in his hand. Then Liz, Steve and Bill got off at the foot of Watson's Hill.

As they reached the level platform outside the dug-out, they heard the raised voices from within. May sounded close to tears, Carl was gruff and Mike's voice was high-pitched such as they had never heard before.

"It's no use you saying, May, that we've *got* to find it!" Mike was shouting, and he never shouted at May, not in this sort of voice, anyway. "It's gone! Gone! Just get that into your head—we've *done* the compressor!"

"Done the compressor!" echoed Bill, pushing through the fly-wire door and down the passageway, nearly knocking a cup of tea out of his mother's hand.

"That's it!" Mike's face was black like the thunder cloud that broke in summer, and he was pressing his lips together over toothless upper gums. "It's gone—stolen! It was gone when Carl and I got out there this morning. Went off overnight . . . I'd like to catch the bloke!"

And it was a good thing that the bloke was not around to be caught, for Mike would surely have hung for murder.

"Have a cup of tea," said May, and thrust the cup hard down on the table. "It'll help you think where else to look."

On the far side of the table Carl picked up the cup that was already in front of him. "Nowhere else to look." He shrugged. "We saw every place today—me and Mike and the mines warden and the police officer. Nowhere else to look."

Carl was of medium height and lean build. His features tended to be long with a strong bone structure, gray eyes well back under heavy brows and drab hair thinning at the temples. Carl was a little younger than Mike and was unmarried. He was a listener rather than a talker. When he did speak—in that very correct English he had learned at school—it was with some authority. He had seen much of life, and not all of it good. As a youth in war-torn Europe, he had learned much.

"But a big thing like a compressor just can't vanish!" argued May, the clip in her hair dangling, her eyes bitter. "A big yellow compressor . . ."

"Not so big," said Carl quietly. "Not a big compressor."

"It cost enough."

"Yes," Carl agreed, "but not big."

"Big or little, you should be able to find it. I'm sure I'd find it!" May was very angry.

Mike snapped then. "You'd better take the ute tomorrow, and see if you can do better than us!"

"We've looked on every field—every diggings," Carl said, his voice quieter and calmer than Mike's, though deeper and gruffer than usual. "And wherever we look, there's a yellow compressor—but not ours. Not one, anyway, that we can say definitely is ours."

"Warden said he can't help any further—nowhere else to look," said Mike.

"And the policeman?"

"Same thing."

"Surely someone saw it go!"

"Not in the dark, and once away from the mine-head it

could be moved openly. These things are constantly being moved about—every time a couple of blokes decide to dig in a different hole."

May sniffed. Probably she would have started to cry if Bill hadn't been there, but it would be embarrassing to cry in front of Bill, who was not one for exposing emotion. "What are you going to do about it?"

"We can't buy another," Mike said. "We'll have to manage until we finish up at Christmas. You and I haven't got four hundred dollars to spend on a compressor, May— and neither has Carl."

"It'll slow you up, Dad," Bill protested quickly.

"Yes—it'll slow us up! And halve our chances, at least!"

"Then borrow some money to buy one—and sell it when you've finished."

May glared at her reckless son. "I'm not agreeing to that! I'm not walking into Grandma Birch's owing money."

"We could stop here—and not have to walk in at all," said Bill, who had to dodge quickly to avoid the stinging flip of a tea towel.

"We'll hire one if we can," Mike said, "but I don't know of any not in use at the moment. It means that you two boys will have to man the winch every weekend—and Carl and I will have to go back to the pick and shovel, cold chisel and hammer." His voice grated. "I'd like to get my hands on that fellow! All I hope, Bill, is that he isn't the father of your friend Nikos."

"Aw, come off it, Dad," Bill said. "Old Melikos is all right. You should listen to him telling stories of the revolution in Greece. How when he was just a kid like Nikos he had to join the Movement and learn to fight . . ."

"I reckon I know he can fight," Mike said glumly.

"They shaved the kids' heads then so that if they were run to ground and someone tried to grab them by the hair there'd be nothing to grip, and they were given slippery uniforms—slippery material, I mean—for the same reason. Must've been great."

"Yes . . . I can imagine!"

"An' he's good at judo and karate—got a Black Belt. He's taught Nikos and Nikos is going to teach me."

"Nikos teach you! He's too fat."

"He can throw me and Steve."

"Well, for goodness' sake, don't get your neck broken before we leave here," muttered May.

Carl stood up then. "Come on, Steve—I've got some stone to clean tonight. If we do get the chance of a compressor on hire, we'll need some handy money."

"I'll be in later to see what that stone's like," Mike said.

May stood up, too, and began to gather up the cups. "I must get on with the sewing as soon as the dishes are done," she said. "Don't want you to arrive in town without a rag to your back, Liz. First impressions are important—and Grandma says there are two boys and a girl next door."

"Older or younger?" Liz asked, not that her thoughts were really with life in town at that moment.

"The girl is your own age—the two boys are sixteen and eighteen. Just the right age for friends. But I want you to look nice when we arrive—not have to hide yourself until we get a few things together. Look—see this style in the *Women's Weekly*? That should suit you. Nice yoke—and I can cut it from the pattern we have."

"Yes, I like that."

"And on this page it tells you how to grow roses. Just look at the pictures. Am I going to grow roses—where there's water and no red dust!" She turned to Mike. "D'ye remember that Lorraine Lee climber we had on the fence of the house we rented in Adelaide when we were first married? I can still smell it. Somehow I can smell it best when the dust here is thick as a fog."

"Yes," said Mike, and his eyes were shadowy as he looked at his wife. Now that her anger had calmed, even the loss of the compressor was secondary to what lay ahead. With Liz growing up, May had changed this last year. Liz was more important to her now—and the learning, and the dresses, and life in town.

"And this page—hairdos. Look, Mike—that's how I'm going to have my hair done. Piled up—and glossy."

"Costs money, doesn't it?"

"Of course it costs money. But d'ye know, I've made up my mind. I'm going to have all this—even if I have to get a job myself. And that won't be hard. There are always part-time typists' jobs for people like me. And Liz'll be able to have more clothes if I work. And she'll need them—just the age to need them."

May wasn't noticing, but Mike's top lip was very tight now over his toothless gum.

"You're not going out to work!" he snarled. "You've helped me, but you've never had to go out to work since we've been married—even if I haven't kept you in silks and satins. And I don't propose that it'll happen in my old age. And have your mother say I can't keep you!"

"But things are going to be different in town," May protested, mildly now. She knew she had been foolish to voice her plans at this moment. "Lots of married women work in town—and how else is Liz going to have what she needs? And me—roses and hairdos?"

"I don't know!" said Mike roughly. "But you can take it from me—I'm still going to wear the pants!"

He flung down the tunnel then to the wire door and swung it wide so roughly that Potch, who was lying outside, caught the edge of it and yelped.

Liz went from the living room into her own small bedroom carved out of the rock. Above her bed she switched on the light which was attached to the flex that ran from the generator. It was a small square room with a low ceiling. A shaft for ventilation went up through the rock at one corner, but it was a long shaft and the wire cover over the top let in very little light, so that she always had to switch on the electric globe.

Her father had made her a strong bookcase that nearly covered the wall opposite her bed. Although she did not possess enough books to fill the shelves, they were stacked high with homemade newspaper scrapbooks and all the odds and ends of a mind that likes to draw knowledge to itself.

The room was neat. On the bed the quilt that May had made was a riot of patchwork colors and there was a posy of artificial flowers on the cheap dressing table. On the wall shelf were some of the toys that Liz retained from early childhood—a couple of dolls, a small brown teddy bear and a procession of china animals. For a child who had had few other children to play with, these were real characters and each one had played its part in the story of her life. She loved them all.

But there were no rock specimens, no stone shells, no pieces of opal. Nothing of opal. For Liz, opal meant only the digging in the ground, the tunnel carrying the weight of the earth, the sweat, the disappointment and the temporary affluence when it was found. Even her mother's ring kindled no fire in her heart.

Now she drew the curtain across the doorway and lay down on the quilt of many colors. She felt miserable and afraid. Her parents did not often row like this. Not this deep-down rowing of two people on different courses— two people who had always traveled the same road. Liz was very afraid. Was a career as a teacher, a life of parties and boyfriends, a going-to-town, worth it? She frowned at the shining specks of gypsum in the ceiling and pretended she didn't hear when her mother called her from the kitchen.

The next three days, too, were worrying ones for Liz. The swimming sports and picnic had been on a Tuesday and for the rest of the week she had to cover up the two boys' after-school activities in the mullock heaps.

This was bad enough, especially as their efforts yielded nothing, but it was made even worse by Bill's constant preoccupation with evolving a "plan" that would not only find opal but the stolen compressor as well.

Some of these ideas—which invariably included her— were so alarming that she was relieved when the weekend came and the two boys were recruited for duty out at the Greek Patch.

5

Spider-Holes of Men

It was just after 6 a.m. the next Saturday morning when Mike started up the utility outside the fly-wire door and turned its nose down the steep slope from the stony platform.

The sky was an immense spread of opal colors—pale blues, greens, rose and red stretched from horizon to horizon, right around the saucer edge of the world. Like a jeweled domed roof the sky rose over the flat earth where occasional sandstone hills protruded like giant burrs.

The earth already was hot, red and dry, and gave no sign that within its depths it secreted the opal whose promise was in the sky.

Carl and Mike rode in the cabin of the utility and Bill, Steve and Potch in the open tray. They had had a good breakfast. Carl had cooked sausages for himself and Steve, and May had put bacon and eggs on the table for Mike and Bill, with lots of toast, and milk in their tea. They had become used to milk since a private airline had been flying it in in cardboard cartons and May was able to transfer it to her kerosene refrigerator. Over the last few years air transport had vastly changed living conditions in the Opal Town. Food was expensive, but there was nothing now that money—if you had it—could not buy.

With the smug little terrier at her feet, May stood at the door and watched them go. May always watched her family off. It was part of her service of love to them, to show that she would be here when they returned.

Liz was not up yet. It was Saturday, and when she was properly awake she would study for an hour or so before getting up. It was just a few weeks now to the exam, and she had to pass or all these plans for next year would be wasted.

And yet, May knew, they had to go to town—whether Liz passed or not—now that Liz was nearing sixteen and Mike forty-four. Liz had to start to live and Mike to readjust before it was too late. It was as simple as that. Liz being clever—and this contingency of having a clever child had never crossed their minds when they tossed that coin —only added weight to that simple fact. But because Mike was Mike, strong and tough at forty-four, and caught on the hook of a windlass, it was so much easier to talk about Liz's education than about the other reasons why it was time to leave the Opal Town.

But May was frowning when she turned, and let the wire door bang shut behind her. Mike was funny about those hairdos and her proposal of going out to work.

The utility growled down the stony slope and onto the wheel tracks that at first crossed and recrossed other wheel tracks, like the lines drawn by the tails of loitering kangaroos, and finally settled to a single line across the flat, through the cleft between the dumps of abandoned diggings and out the nine miles to the Greek Patch.

The track was carved deep into two single wheel grooves, the edges spiked with tire-tearing sandstone. Yet they traveled fast. Only the newcomers—for the first few weeks—nursed their tires and their undercarriage on these devils' tracks.

It was a flat track on a flat surface, and isolated along the miles were bare whitening dumps, like horny callouses on the red ground, where men had tried their luck. They were silent tombstones to dead hope.

The Greek Patch, large and somewhat straggling, could be seen from some distance off. This man-made collection of hillocks looked like a loose cluster of low flat-topped pyramids and, like the opal, were of rainbow colors— mauves, pinks, creamy yellows—depending on what had gone into the formation of the sandstone brought up from beneath the earth's surface. No weed, not even the annual saltbush, grew on these dumps which turned out to be not pyramids but the walls of the spider-holes of men.

Until the utility actually entered the field there was no sign of life, and the only noise was the thick chugging of the engine grinding across the gibbers. There were many gaping and idle shafts, some abandoned in disappointment, some denuded of their riches, and around these rejected diggings not even the flies buzzed. Scattered around were old castoff hand windlasses, rusting oil drums and the weathered pegs of abandoned claims.

Then they passed a tent or two and an occasional galvanized iron shack with the roof held down with rocks. There were no suitable hills for dugouts here, and those miners who liked to live on the job were content with this poor shelter.

Here and there was a man at work on top of his spider-hole, winch turning, usually to the tune of the phut-phut of the diesel but sometimes silently, powered only by muscles.

It was named the Greek Patch because a Greek, or rather a Greek "company," had made the first find here. It had been a big find—a quarter of a million dollars for the ten men involved.

That was a point about the Greeks. They worked together and grub-staked each newcomer until he had found enough opal to support himself. Certainly he had to repay whatever he cost his benefactors, but at least he knew he would be supported until he could pay.

And when they were on promising ground, they strung a number of claims together—each claim being the permitted 150 feet by 150 feet—so that if the lead or trace led beyond the boundary, it could be picked up again in the next claim. By this method they made some rich finds.

But sometimes different "companies" really meant different feuding families, and if one was getting opal and the other not, then a bullet might whizz through a tin shack; while underground, men might "infiltrate" into the others' legal claim.

Australians seldom worked in companies or large teams. It was every man for himself—staking and working his own claim, generally with a team of three as the limit.

There were not many Australians on this field—just an isolated mine here and there for, somehow, it had come to be regarded as Greek territory. But it was a spot on this field that Mike had got his hunch about.

It had happened one day during the winter months when he had been carting a load of firewood from twenty miles out—the nearest source of supply—and the tailboard of the utility had slipped and part of his load tumbled out.

Such a thing had never happened before. The tailboard was usually stiff to move. At the same time, directly overhead in the sunset sky was a single small round cloud painted by the sun to look like a perfect polished gem of fiery opal; and that night Mike had dreamed of both—the mulga firewood and the opal cloud.

Mike wasn't given to fantasy. But because he and Carl had just suffered the disappointment of losing a promising lead, he had gone out to the Greek Patch the very next day and staked a claim on the spot where the mulga had hit the ground beneath the cloud of opal. He had pegged out the full amount of ground permitted to himself and Carl and May—the manpower clause of May's claim being covered by the machinery they had in use.

This spot was just beyond the last of the dumps on the far edge of the field.

That was four weeks ago now and their main shaft was down seventy feet to the fourth level. If they were going to stay in this hole it was time to register it. Like all miners they didn't want to do this until they were certain the hole was worth it.

Mike had christened it *Eldorado*, much to May's irritation. "With a name like that it can't help but fail," she declared.

But they had found trace and some opal on each level and put in a number of drives, the yield being enough to cover their overhead expenses—a "wages" claim.

Today, as they emerged near Eldorado from the narrow track between the dumps and shafts, Bill saw Nikos standing on top of a mound to the left, directly opposite Eldorado. The boy was unhooking a bucket of stone from the winch and pushing it along the skid pole, greased with fat, to empty at the outer edge of the mound.

Pappa Melikos was squatting on his haunches on the ground at the side of the dump. He was measuring even lengths of yellow fuse and snipping them off with pliers, ready for the charges. They were long lengths—six feet at least—which meant they were going to let off a number of shots together. A box of gelignite lay under the shelter of a sheet of iron at his side. He didn't look up as the Watsons' utility went by, and Nikos gave only a half-hearted wave to Bill's friendly call.

But that was like Nikos. He was always a bit stand-offish when his father was about. The old man was boss. Nikos had told him that a Greek father demanded, and received, explicit obedience from a son until he married, even if the son was thirty. As Nikos could see no prospect of being married until he grew up, and Pappa was a holder of a Black Belt, he found it a long prospect.

So Bill understood that half-hearted wave.

That was when Bill noticed that there was another shaft, with a number of men working, running parallel to but in between that of Melikos and Eldorado. The men were Greeks but he didn't recognize any of their faces. They were newcomers. Perhaps Pappa Melikos had taken on new "company" and was sinking a new shaft.

Mike pulled up with a great rattle of stones at the side of their own dump. From the top of the winch straddling their shaft flew the scarlet pennant with which Mike always liked to identify his mine.

The motorized winch was the modern counterpart of the hand windlass and allowed the use of the twenty-two-gallon drum in place of the twelve-gallon bucket. Machinery—some of it costing thousands of dollars—was essential in up-to-date opal mining, and that was why the absence of the yellow compressor which should have flanked the dump was so bitterly depressing.

Bill saw his father eye the spot where it should have been, and saw his brows draw tight.

"Should have got out here a bit earlier—those Greeks don't waste any time," Mike said gruffly, the heavy frown revealing the kind of thoughts he had toward *that* fellow —if only he could get his hands on him. That he was in a mood to deal out a swift and summary justice to the culprit was certain. And even Bill knew that this could be dangerous on the opal field.

"They're workers—especially the new gang," agreed Carl, his tone even. He was philosophical now about the compressor, and was prepared to be patient until there was one for hire. "I've never seen a shaft go down so quickly."

"They've got the manpower!" Mike said shortly, and turned to hammer down a loose piece of the timbering around the shaft head. The sandstone walls of a shaft required no shoring up, but sometimes the red topsoil and the loose jasper just beneath it, as well as the rubble of the ever-rising dump, had to be strengthened. This was done by spreading flattened cardboard cartons from the store over the loose material and battening them down with any available bits of wood.

As Mike straightened up he said, "We'd better get started."

Before knock-off time the previous afternoon the two

men had let off thirty fractures. This was their usual practice so that the poisonous fumes of the gelignite had time to clear by the next morning. When this was not convenient, and provided there was a good wind, they used the explosive just before the midday break, turning the opening of the air sock, which was a long calico funnel going down the depth of the shaft, into the wind current and relying on this device to clear the air below.

"We've got a lot of stone to pull," Mike now said, "but the two of you on the winch should be able to handle the big buckets. Carl and I will give you a rest every now and then."

Neither Bill nor Steve minded being on the winch. They were tough-muscled, used to work, and if Steve wasn't as interested in opal as Bill, he still liked to work beside his mate.

They lowered Mike down on the "chair," or sling, and then Carl. The chair was a piece of iron about a foot long and three inches wide, turned up a couple of inches at either end, with a wire loop for a belt around the body. The miner could sit or stand on his chair but, either way, he dangled like a spider on the end of its web.

For safety's sake—if the motorized winch failed—there was a ladder, in six foot lengths that hooked one on to the other, down the side of the shaft to a convenient height from the seventy-foot bottom.

Soon the warning bell on top of the winch tingled that the first bucket was ready, and Bill pushed the lever. As the bucket reached the top, Steve helped him grab the heavy load and slide it along the skid pole, then tip at the edge of the dump.

"Bit of potch in there," Bill said, eyes brightening. "Not bad-looking stuff."

"That'll only tantalize your dad," Steve said. "It's the real thing he wants—not potch."

"It's still good trace," Bill declared. He slipped the empty oil drum back on the safety hook—a hook with an extra turn on the tip like Potch's tail—and lowered away.

It was as the bucket bottomed and he straightened up that he noticed the cigarette butt. It was lying among the stone just beyond the top of the ladder.

Evidently his own feet, pressing hard to move the load, had shifted the rubble enough to reveal the stub. His mouth tightened instantly. His father didn't smoke at all, and Carl only a pipe.

"Look!" he pointed. "We've had a visitor."

"Yeah . . ." Steve stared down.

"And close to the ladder! Someone could have been down the mine. Dad'll explode!"

The boys looked at each other, then Bill bent down to examine the butt more closely while Steve sat back on his haunches, the muscles of his legs rounding. "Don't tell him," he said.

"Don't tell him! Why?"

"What's the good?" Steve's big dark eyes were quiet, and something of the passiveness of his race was there. "He's mad now—he could do something pretty silly. In any case, it could have been the mines warden—he smokes—or the copper. They were probably all over the mine head, looking for clues, the day the compressor went."

"Could explain it," Bill conceded.

But he still frowned, and Steve went on. "Even if someone has been down, what would they see? Mike and Carl haven't found anything specially good."

That was true. And no doubt Steve, who never seemed to burn with sudden and wasteful anger, was right. A cigarette butt that had most likely belonged to the warden or the policeman was hardly worth offering to his father as fuel for *his* anger.

"Reckon you're right . . ." he muttered, but even so he took a hefty kick at a stone.

There was a yell from below—"What d'ye think you're doing up there! Throwing confetti?"—and a pull on the bell for the load to come up.

Up and down went the twenty-two-gallon bucket with its two hundredweight of stone. Steve and Bill operated the lever and emptied the load until their arms worked automatically, until their wet singlets were cast down beside them and their sweating backs glowed from a brilliant sun in a sky that was now a bright blue.

While they worked Potch lay on the stones not far from them. Once two barefooted Aboriginal women, clad in shapeless cotton dresses discolored with red dust and carrying their gin bars, moved in to noodle on a distant dump. They were followed by a group of children and two dogs at heel, which caused Potch to shift restlessly and creep nearer the skid pole.

Just before lunchtime they listened to the dull measured boom—one shot following the other—of blasting from both nearby shafts. It was close enough to rattle the stones around their own mine head.

And so on through the long hot day.

In the afternoon Mike and Carl made ready another batch of charges, and after lighting them and counting each explosion to make sure all had gone off, they climbed into the utility and set off homeward.

They had worked a little later than usual, and the Melikos men had already gone.

Sunday began with the same pattern, much to May's annoyance. Sunday was usually the one day of the week when Mike and Carl did not go out to the mine. In fact, few miners worked on Sunday, particularly the Greeks, among whom a superstition had grown up that it was unlucky to work on Sunday. This was because, among them, there had been two or three fatal mine accidents on a Sunday.

In any case, most miners found it more convenient to work only six days a week, for there was always a bit of washing to do, the week's food supplies to get in and gelignite to be bought from the Miners' Store. The store sold the explosive a little cheaper on Sundays, to save bringing it from the safety dump, half a mile away, on more than one day of the week.

But May was cross because she had planned a midday roast dinner. This was what her mother used to do on Sunday, and as they would soon be going back to live like ordinary folks she had decided to make a start on these customary habits.

However, Mike and Carl insisted that, as they needed the boys' help and it could only be given at the weekend, they had to make the most of it. They would be just as happy to eat the roast dinner at night as at midday.

So they set off at the same early hour.

The Greek Patch was quiet when they arrived, with scarcely a miner working and Melikos and his men absent. Their absence seemed to put Mike in a better humor and he went down the shaft with a half-whistle trying to pucker out from that toothless upper gum.

Then the work was on. For those first few early hours
the boys had little time to get their breath between buckets. The men were working with a concentration of energy
that kept the winch turning.

But as lunchtime drew near, the time lapse between
buckets began to grow longer and the warning bell tinkled
less frequently.

"They're getting tired," said Bill. "Reckon it's time they
came up and did a turn on the winch."

The men came up soon after, and Bill saw at once that
his father's mood had indeed changed, that he was excited
and that his hand shook as he took a swig at the water bottle. Carl's movements were quicker than usual—the way
he sprang off the chair, sending a shower of pebbles below,
the way he almost ran to the utility for the tucker-bag.

"How are you going?" Bill demanded, his questing eye
going from one man to the other.

"The trace is good," Mike said, not looking at his son.

But Bill was quick. "Very good, eh? Can I go down and
look?"

Mike hesitated.

"Better let him go," Carl said. "We won't shake him off
now."

"I suppose you're right," Mike agreed. "It's on the left-
hand side of the drive, Bill."

Bill looked at his mate. "Coming, Steve?"

The dark boy hesitated. The spider-tunnels held no at-
traction for him and his skin turned clammy in the coolness down there. He never went underground voluntarily,
but he never refused Bill anything, either, so he grinned
and said, "Yep."

Mike lowered each of them down the seventy feet. At
the bottom of the shaft they picked up the electric light

globe in its wire guard and on a long flex from the thirty-two-volt generator above.

The drive was already a good thirty feet in from the shaft and would soon necessitate another air vent, but it was over five feet in height and they didn't have to stoop too much as they went slowly along, carefully examining the sandstone face.

Then they came upon it. First just a feathery line of milky-looking potch wavering through the sandstone, but bulging here and there with the irregularity of its crevice. Then suddenly it was potch with color—and, in a tiny pocket, pure color! It looked like red banked fire as the electric light washed over it. A pocket of gem opal—precious opal. Just a tiny pocket, but precious opal.

"Ste-eve!" Bill gasped. "Looks as though they've struck it."

"Only a tiny pocket . . ." Steve cautioned. "Then it's potch again—see?"

"Where there's color like that, there'll be more!" Bill was confident. "Gosh—this could be *the* lead!"

Steve grinned, but he wasn't excited like Bill because the stone itself held little interest for him. The most perfect specimen ever unearthed would never be more than a pretty stone to him, though neither would it be a "debbil-debbil" stone—as it was to some of the older Aborigines who, it would seem, regarded those living colors as imprisoned dancing spirits. But Steve could thrill to what it might mean to his friends.

He waved a hand at the wall. "The trace goes straight on—almost horizontal—toward the north boundary of the claim."

"Yes, that's how it looks, and this could be the pointer

they've been hoping for!" Bill agreed eagerly. "Though of course you never can tell—it might go down, or it could double back."

"Mike and Carl will know," Steve assured him. "They know these things and they will work it out. Now we'd better go up. Your dad said not to be long."

They gave the signal and Steve was hauled up first, then Bill. As soon as Bill reached eye level he saw that, in the meantime, some of the men had arrived at the new shaft, though neither Nikos nor Melikos was among them. He tried to get off the sling as casually as possible. As he landed his father warned him, "Take it quietly, Bill—your pals have got their eyes on us. One bit of excitement and they'll twig what's here."

"Do you think they've come out to work, Dad?"

"Not in the mine. They seem to be busy with some repairs to their buckets and gear. Now, start your lunch."

So Bill and Steve each dived a hand into the tucker-bag and commenced to munch in unison with the two men. To further conceal their excitement they ate their lunch slowly, and this also allowed some quiet discussion on their next moves.

"This break couldn't have come at a better time," Mike told the boys, munching with great enjoyment. "We have to register Eldorado tomorrow. I can hardly believe we've been working in this hole for four weeks and we've been wondering whether we should abandon the south section in favor of taking up the square on our north boundary. What we've uncovered this morning seems to be saying 'Go north.' What d'ye think, Carl?"

Carl frowned and chewed steadily for a moment. "This is always the problem—which way? Which way is the run going to go? This is the thing we pray to know." Then he gave the biggest, widest grin that Bill had ever seen on that serious face. "This time we *do* know—north."

"Considering the position of the slide and that horizontal run, I reckon it must," Mike said happily. "So, tomorrow—as we can't *add* to the ground we've got—we'll abandon the south section and extend to the north."

"Ja." Carl lit his pipe and puffed comfortably.

Mike looked across to the new shaft where the men were still busy with their surface tasks but obviously not intending to go underground. His eyes narrowed. "We won't waste any time about it," he said, suddenly edgy. "We'll register with the mines warden first thing in the morning."

Carl followed his gaze and nodded.

"In the meantime," Mike went on, "to hoodwink that company, we'll work the rest of today to our usual pattern. Except—you'll have to pry loose that bit of color, Carl."

Again Carl nodded and said, "Ja."

So when they had finished their lunch, the two men were lowered once more into the mine and the buckets of stone began to come up again. Not as fast as when they had started the morning's work, but at regular intervals. The boys knew what was going on. Carl would be gouging delicately at that bright seam through the sandstone and Mike would be filling the bucket with rubble and wheeling it on the flat bucket-barrow to the bottom of the shaft.

Not that Mike couldn't pick carefully when he had to, but Carl was even more careful, more controlled. He wouldn't spoil or lose a single gem, and Mike was content for his partner to do this deliberate picking while he did the rough labor.

The two men hoped that they would be able to finish

work at their usual time—mainly because to work beyond that hour would tell its own story of discovery, of excitement, of reluctance to leave the shaft—but neither did they want to leave a speck of gem opal flashing from that rock face. So as soon as the last piece fell, they filled their pockets, instead of the usual calico bags, with the stones and signaled to be brought up.

They were surprised to find that it was already dark but also relieved to be told that the Greek company had left a couple of hours earlier. Nevertheless, although they were going home with such hopeful news to May and her roast dinner, Mike's hard driving showed that he hadn't quite rid himself of that edginess.

6

The Opal Cutter

As IT turned out, Carl and Steve didn't join the Watsons over that Sunday evening dinner table. It was Carl's task to do the initial cleaning of the opal and he was anxious to start on the stones they had just brought back from Eldorado. So he and Steve headed straight for their own dugout.

Carl's dugout contained only three small compartments, one behind the other. The kitchen-living room led directly into the bedroom which Carl and Steve shared and which, in turn, led to Carl's workroom. The furniture was sparse. In the living room were a couple of chairs, a table, portagas stove, refrigerator and a shelf for Carl's pipes and tobacco; in the bedroom were two beds, a chest of drawers and a wardrobe made by hanging a curtain from a wooden frame across the corner.

There was linoleum on the stone floor which was swept every day, and the aluminum kettle was kept shining. There were no artificial flowers, but there were white sheets and pillowcases beneath the gray blankets on the beds, and clothes were always hung up. Carl had been brought up by a strict mother to respect good living, and he wouldn't leave the dugout in the morning until the beds were made and the dishes washed.

The clothes hanging under that wardrobe cover were clean, too. Every Sunday—except a Sunday such as today, when they had to work at the mine—Carl did the washing. Rather, now that Steve was getting older, he instructed Steve how to use the small washing machine and how to press the khaki shorts or the cotton jeans or the shirts they wore. No boy went to school looking cleaner than Steve.

The boy was fortunate that it was Carl who had befriended him when his mother died so soon after his father had been gored fatally by a bull. The Aboriginal woman had come into the Opal Town from Water-Hole Creek Station to noodle a living for her son, because the father had said, as he lay dying, that she must always earn her way as he had done, and she must see, too, that the boy went to school. The Opal Town had the only school in thousands of square miles.

It hadn't been easy for her. Her husband had traveled overseas to fight with the Rats of Tobruk, had known what the wide world was like and had found a place in it, but she knew only the world of the cattle station and the near-desert and the Opal Town. But, for as long as she could, she had lived in the town and looked after her son as the older Steve had taught her.

When she died, Carl had taken the quiet Aboriginal boy to live with him. Steve had learned to use toothpaste, to keep his boots shining and to slick down his hair with oil as Carl did.

Carl's workroom was just as neat and orderly as the rest of his dugout. It was scarcely larger than a cubbyhole, with no direct air shaft, and it was a black cubbyhole if the generator was not working. Strangely enough, this living in a hole in the hillside did not trouble Steve, perhaps because it did not go *down* like a shaft.

On the two walls at either side of the entrance were workbenches. On one Carl had set up a power-driven opal saw and grinding and polishing wheels; the other was for cleaning and sorting the stone.

Above the second bench was a shelf on which stood a row of "specimens"—all kinds of unusual stone and opalized formations that, over many years, Carl had dug up from the earth's depths. There was a "painted lady," a piece of matrix blended with all the colors of the spectrum. There were sea shells, opalized to an incredible bluish-green and set fast in rock. There was a slab of white sandstone about a foot long and eight inches high, so impregnated with brilliant veins of fiery green-red opal and intersected with the brown dye streaks of ironstone that it looked like a slab of rainbow cake.

This piece mocked with its imprisoned wealth, for the opal was so diffused through the rock as to make its removal impossible without fracturing and destroying its value and beauty forever. But Carl loved it because it defied being broken up and graded and sold. Like May with her ring, he would have to be starving before he sold this specimen.

Carl was sitting at his bench now. In front of him was the small parcel of stones which they had carried from Eldorado in their pockets. He was snipping carefully at each piece—fractured and made separate and different from all the other pieces millions of years ago. Had he bothered to lay each one flat on the table he could have fitted them into a whole, like the parts of a perfect jigsaw puzzle.

He used his pliers with deft and accurate fingers, clipping along one edge so that, when offered to a buyer, the latter could see the quality of the gem before making his offer.

Steve, and Bill as well now, were watching him.

They were taking up what little space there was in the workroom. This was one reason why Bill had rushed from the family dinner table as quickly as he could. Soon his mother, father and Liz would be in to know how the stone was measuring up, and there would be no room for him and Steve.

In any case, he had been glad to get away from all the plans that were being made at home and all the excitement. Mum and Liz were acting as though *already* a big parcel had been found.

His mother had at once decided that they would now be able to afford a house with five bedrooms—the extra two being for their friends—on the beach front at Glenelg, with a tennis court and private swimming pool. She would have a permanent booking with the hairdresser, and she wouldn't sew any more—Liz would look a dream in really well-made clothes; while Bill could go to the grammar school and learn to be a gentleman, and Mike needn't worry about a job—he could take up bowls to fill in *his* time.

When he could get a word in, Mike had pointed out that what they had found today was only an indication.

"Might lead to nothing further—it's happened before."

"Of course it's happened before," May agreed cheer-

fully, "but I know what you're thinking, Mike Watson—
that this *is* it. Don't forget that this spot was your hunch—
where the mulga fell right under that cloud of opal."

"I'm not forgetting." Mike grinned. "But the trace is
horizontal and heading for the north boundary. We just
have to hope that by extending our claim to the next block
on the north—which means giving up one section of what
we've already pegged—we'll contain it. The whole has to
be registered by tomorrow, May, and I can tell you—I'll
be on the doorstep of that mines warden's office when it
opens in the morning!"

And May said, "I just didn't expect the parcel with our
name on it to turn up so quickly."

That was when Bill had hurried off because, somehow,
even the parcel with their name on it and the house at
Glenelg—with a bedroom for Steve—and the grammar
school for him and bowls for his father suddenly looked a
black prospect indeed.

Grammar school—gentleman . . . He hated the city.
The people always looked unhappy, hurrying along the
streets, heads down, not interested in anyone else but
themselves and never friendly. If a bloke smiled at someone, just in passing, they thought he was a nong and ought
to be locked up. And that grammar school! He squirmed.

He couldn't listen to his mother and Liz.

But when Potch followed him, tipping his leg with his
wet nose, the resentment died. At least Potch could go
with them to their own home, and Steve would be there.
After all, these were the things that mattered.

So he cheered up, and hurried to see what Carl was
doing with the stone.

The two boys watched his snip-snipping. He went along only one side, licking the raw edge to bring up the color so that he could decide to which quality it belonged—first, second, third, fourth, even fifth—at least, as he judged it. Not that he was always right. Mike was really the classer. Mike's fingers were not as "soft" as Carl's for this handling, but he was seldom wrong when it came to classifying and many of the miners on the field brought their stones to him to classify.

When selling the rough opal, the miner found it a help in bargaining to have some idea of the value of his "parcel." A buyer came to the Opal Town with possibly fifty thousand dollars in cash in his pocket. He visited the miners in their dugouts or in their mines. They sparred with each other a little before the miner, as a rule, would even admit he had opal to sell. Then they would sit on either side of a table, the parcel before them, and the buyer would say, "How much do you want?"

And the miner would shrug and say, "What d'ye offer?"

If the offer was more than he expected, he might, with an appropriate show of reluctance, close the deal right then, but if the offer was less, he would stick out for his price, depending, of course, on how long it was since he had found his last parcel and how full his larder. But to have a reliable estimate of the value was to be forearmed, so Mike was always in great demand as a classer.

So the little piles that Carl was making now would be gone over later by Mike with a sharp eye.

Steve was sitting at the one open end of the bench on a three-legged stool, leaning forward on folded arms, the sleeves of his red and gray checked shirt rolled above his elbows. Now and again his dark eyes smiled, and he said, "Good bit—eh?"

"Ja—good bit."

Sometimes Carl would place that piece in an isolated pile at his elbow. This was the very small percentage that he was reserving to be cut and polished for the town's tourist trade. He would say, "It will cut a solid. You can cut that piece, Steve."

Then he would go on snipping while the boy grinned. Steve enjoyed cutting and polishing the precious stone, mainly because he liked to be told he had "soft" fingers. Sometimes he looked at them, wondering about this "feel" that he was told he had. Carl had given much time to teaching him to cut opal, and said he would always be able to get work as an opal cutter.

But Steve was glad Carl hadn't tried to change his decision to enter the Police Force. After all, opal was only a bit of rock, but a policeman was someone with authority, with standing. Steve hoped he had a "feel" for being a policeman, too.

He wanted to look well in his uniform, too, as his father had done in his soldier's uniform. That was why he walked so straight when he went to school, wore boots because Carl said he must train his feet now and was happy to work with the men so that his muscles would be strong.

It was Bill now who waved a hand at the bits of stone. "This afternoon's find is going to lead to something pretty good—eh?"

Carl laid down both snips and opal to look at the boy, his lean face very long and his gray eyes very quiet.

"Could be. So much so that I'm telling you—both of you—that if there'd been any way of hiding developments from you, we'd have done so."

Bill thrust out his chin. "You're a bit tough. When have Steve and I ever given anything away?"

"In the past there's been nothing much to give away," Carl said mildly, "but this time could be different. This new Greek friend of yours, for instance . . ."

Bill's face went hot. "Nikos is all right," he said roughly. "D'ye think I'd open my trap?"

"Just warning you—both of you," Carl picked up his snips again, taking the merest edge off a stone as big as a ten-cent piece and still lightly coated with sandstone. As he put it down carefully in the little pile that both boys knew were "firsts," a red-green fire started from the revealed edge.

"It is good!" Bill cried.

"If there's enough of it—and if we've made the right choice of direction—it could be very good," Carl said.

7

Too Late!

MIKE was very restless for the remainder of that Sunday night. The day's developments had offered rich possibilities but also had engendered a needling impatience.

Neither he nor Carl had been concerned to register their pegged claims until the termination of the thirty days allowed by the Mines Department. With finances low, there was no point in paying the ten-dollar registration fee —which gave a twelve-month lease of the claim—until they were certain that that piece of ground would go on yielding opal.

And while Eldorado had been promising, it had offered nothing definite until today. Today it had not only revealed rich promise but also the disturbing fact that the "run" could continue north beyond their present boundary!

So Mike was restless and impatient for the morning and the registering of the claims. He hardly listened to May when she told him that, although she hadn't been able to

74

cook the roast dinner at midday, she had followed some of the pattern of town living by tuning into the radio church broadcast. It had had to be radio because there was no church in the Opal Town other than the little mission church attended mainly by the Aborigines.

And that had made her think, she said, how nice it would be next year when Liz and Bill would go to church regularly and join the youth groups and the tennis club. That would mean two rackets—but of course they would be able to afford them now—and nice white shorts and a tennis dress. A flared dress, she thought, with lace panties underneath, would be very nice. She would enjoy seeing Liz going off looking so attractive.

And though Mike wasn't really listening, he smiled and nodded his head. He knew that May chattered on because she was excited, too.

On that Monday morning, Mike rose at the usual time, determined that he and Carl would be first in line for the warden's attention, not that any business would be conducted before 8:30 A.M. The mines warden was a lean, shrewd, blue-eyed man, always dressed in khaki cotton slacks, khaki shirt and wide felt hat, yet always looking as though the sun had got at him. He was the most obliging, understanding, conciliatory man on the field, provided he didn't have to register claims or settle disputes before 8:30 A.M. He was most unlikely to answer the doorbell before that time and would swear at anyone who rang it.

Mike did not mind the prospect of a long wait, but he did want to be first.

"It's lucky that we can register a claim in your name, May," he said, shaking his head at the offer of a second cup of tea, "and an extra lucky break that we know just where we want it. Without a doubt that run is heading north."

May was unlikely these days to turn a winch or fill a bucket, but she was entitled to register a claim if she wanted—provided someone, or the equivalent machinery, did the work—that would secure the permitted area on the north boundary of Eldorado.

"Another five years," Bill put in, "and I'll be able to register a claim, too."

"You'll be a city slicker by then," said May with great satisfaction, "and you'll have forgotten what a shaft looks like!"

"You're hoping!" said Bill rudely.

Then Mike went out to start up the utility. They heard him buzz the starter for a while, but there was no answering response from the engine. Then they heard Carl join him, and more buzzing. But still the engine didn't buzz into life.

As May had to sign the registration form for her claim, she was dressed ready to accompany the two men and now she and Bill went out to investigate, leaving Liz still eating her breakfast, with a red-covered British history textbook propped up in front of her.

"Reckon we'll have to push her down the hill," Mike said. "She'll start then—must've been a bit cold last night."

"Plugs might need cleaning," Carl said. "I'll do them when we get back from the warden."

Mike waved a hand at his son. "Here, Bill—help push down the slope." Mike was wearing a shirt with his shorts this morning and his teeth were in his mouth instead of in the cup on the sink.

So Carl and Bill, soon joined by Steve, pushed the vehicle while Mike sat behind the wheel ready to let out the clutch at the crucial moment. But beyond a series of coughs from the engine nothing had developed by the time the flat track at the bottom of the slope was reached.

By then Mike was angry and red-faced. "What can be the matter with the thing?" he shouted. "Never stuck us up like this before!"

"Sounds as though it's out of petrol," said Carl.

"I filled her when we got back from the field yesterday. Can't be out!"

But Carl already had the petrol cap off, his eye to the hole and his arm rocking the tank for the glint of liquid movement. He straightened quickly. "Dry as a bone—not a drop in her!"

"Can't be!" Mike looked at his partner with disbelieving eyes. Then he rocked the tank and put his eye to the hole, and he, too, straightened with a jerk. "You're right—dry as a bone. Well—we'll have to fill her up!"

He turned and took the slope up to the platform in a running stride.

The drum of petrol was housed on the outside right of the platform, and Mike soon had filled a handy can. A couple of cans, he judged, would be ample to get as far as the warden's office and back. Then once again he climbed into the driver's seat, Carl and May beside him, and pressed the starter. There was one sputter of life, and again the engine died. Several sputters—with the same result.

"Dirt in the carburetor," Carl said with finality. "Using the starter with the tank empty has drawn it through."

Mike grated the hated teeth. "That means we'll have to walk!" And he flung at May, "And walk quickly!"

May recognized the urgent note and hurried after the two men.

"Never again will we be caught with only one vehicle in commission!" Mike said grimly. "That old car of yours, May, will go up to the workshop for new gears this afternoon!"

Before turning onto the road, May paused to call up the slope. "Liz, don't forget the clock—or you'll be late for school!"

Bill turned to say to Steve, "We might as well walk along with them. Let's get our books."

They both set off up the slope in long hops like two young kangaroos, though Bill stopped for a split second just at the top to bend and pick up an object from the ground and put it into his pocket before racing in for his schoolbag.

Steve looked at him questioningly when he joined him again but Bill appeared not to notice, so Steve knew that he mustn't ask questions with all the grownups about but would be told later. Then they set off after their elders.

Three white adults walking so hard along the stony track was a most unusual sight for the Opal Town, especially at that early hour. From every utility and car that passed on its way out to the various fields came a remark, laughing, wondering, derisive, and Mike was hard-pushed not to shout back rudely.

"That petrol didn't leak out!" he fumed. "Someone milked the tank during the night. And Potch didn't bark— must have known who it was."

Carl didn't answer, but his lips were tight around the stem of his pipe from which there came no waft of smoke. May didn't answer, either. From tennis outfits to milked tanks was a long stride.

The warden's house also contained his office, as well as being the official residence of the policeman. It was a small weatherboard house, and one of the few permanent buildings—which included the two stores, school, teachers' residences, hospital, mission church and motel—above ground. This permanent house was built on the surface because the government could afford to transport materials hundreds of miles to the spot and provide an air-conditioning unit run by the diesel motor that stood in the back yard.

The house was planted squarely on the flat edge of the tableland and was fenced in with a square wire fence. Fifty yards away stood the lockup—a tin shed less than half the size of an ordinary garage, with no window, a big padlock on the door and a revolving fan on top to drive air down to anyone who might be incarcerated. There was no fence around it.

From this rise, the haze of morning softened the stretch of flat below and the slopes of the far edge of the plateau into a wide still canvas done in pastels, reds and blues, but no green—green was always missing from this country except for a short period immediately after rain. Here and there a vehicle was chugging softly like a distant motorboat, rocking on the wavy tracks. The westerly and the dust had not yet risen and the haze was peaceful.

But as the three grownups turned in at the cyclone-wire gates, Bill and Steve just behind, the peace disappeared with a bang like a charge of gelignite. For though it wasn't yet half-past eight, there was already a group of men waiting for the front door to open. There was an Australian, several Italians and four Greeks, the latter from the shaft between that of Melikos and Eldorado. The Greeks were the first in the line.

Containing his anger with great difficulty, Mike had to accept his position on the tail end.

Bill and Steve ambled just around the corner of the building, pretending to be interested in the police Land Rover stabled in the car annex. The young policeman who had come to do his four months' duty in the area was a pleasant fellow and, with Steve planning to join the force, there was surely excuse enough for their interest. From here, too, they could hear and see whatever developed without being right under their elders' feet. They knew how elders hated to have them underfoot when things were happening.

Every now and again a waxbill flew above their heads to its nest along the rafters. There were half a dozen nests, all made in wide-lipped, flat camp-pie tins which the warden himself had nailed there several seasons ago after the first pair of birds had arrived, obviously distressed at finding neither place nor materials for a nest. In the past, there had been a little mulga about the Opal Town and apparently the birds had come back looking for it. Now they still returned each year, and when one tin rusted away the warden quietly put up another. Not even the young policeman dared ask him why he did it, or who kept the dish of water filled at the side of the house.

The warden was slow with his interviews this morning. Perhaps there were some complaints being lodged, which always took time, or maybe some of the new fellows were having language difficulties explaining just where their claims were.

At last it was the Watsons' and Carl's turn. But they hadn't been in the office very long when the two boys heard angry voices. They couldn't hear what was said but Bill knew that his father's voice was among them.

"Sounds hopping mad!" he whispered to Steve.

"He does!"

A few minutes later May came out followed by the two men. They spoke no word until they were beyond the wire fence that enclosed the stony plot.

"Dad . . . ?" Bill asked, knowing that the news was not good.

"Those Greeks—blast 'em!" Mike said. "They got in first! They've each registered a claim on all four sides of us —including the north! They've pegged us in! It's a wonder they didn't go for Eldorado itself—but I guess they weren't quite game enough to do that." His arms sagged a little as though he was suddenly tired, and he looked at his wife. "There won't be any five-bedroom house in Glenelg, May. It's Grandma Birch's—for sure!"

It was then that Bill's fingers clasped like a vise over the hard object in his pocket—a stone fan shell. A very good specimen—but with a chip out of the top of the fan—like the one Nikos had found on the day of the picnic.

8

Kathy's News

BILL scuffed through the red dust and the stones and the dry wind. He knew he shouldn't scuff—thongs wore out quickly enough on the stones—but the wind, which he always found exciting, was stronger than usual and there was no grass on which to walk. In fact there was not a green blade anywhere, except for the single sunflower plant, tall and not yet ripe, that grew at the side of the Opal Town Store where the waste-water pipe dripped out onto the red earth. It was a fortunate seed to have fallen in such a position. Of all those that must have blown from the two plants that Old Welhelm had nurtured at the door of his dugout last year, apparently this was the only one to have found a drop of moisture.

Grass . . . Bill didn't know why he thought of grass—he hadn't seen any since their last visit to Adelaide, which was two years ago. He remembered that the grass had been in neat squares and tidy as a geometrical pattern. Then he suddenly realized why he was thinking of grass. It was because of what his father had said this morning after leaving the mines warden's office, about going to live with Grandma Birch *for sure.* Her lawn was very square. Bill could still hear his father's hoarse, "Pegged in on all sides!"

It was at that stage that he and Steve had turned quickly toward the school which shared this edge of the tableland with the warden's house. There had been no point in remaining with the grownups to hear more of the disaster. There would be nothing to hear but bitter words, and Carl swearing in German. That was always interesting, of course—Carl swearing in German, thinking they didn't understand what he said.

Now school was over for the day and Bill was on his way home. He was alone because Steve had had to remain in the classroom while Mr. Robbins went over some arithmetic with him. And this was a pity, as there was just a possibility that Nikos would be waiting for them at the first bulldozer cutting out on the flat. The cutting was their permanent meeting place. As often as possible, when Melikos brought his company in from the mine early in the afternoon, Nikos would wait for Bill there.

But would he be there today? Would he dare to be there after milking the ute and delaying Mike's getting to the mines warden's office before those Greek newcomers?

Bill wished that Steve was with him. There hadn't been much opportunity through the day to discuss what they should do with Nikos. Nikos—who they had believed wanted their friendship. They had talked about it a little at lunchtime, but without getting beyond relieving their feelings.

"We could beat him up!" Bill said fiercely. "We could

kidnap him and demand a ransom from old Melikos—a big ransom, enough to cover what they'll get out of those claims. We could take him out into the mulga and lose him—and find him when the reward's big enough!"

"I reckon—as a future policeman—I should warn you," Steve said, "this would be against the law—and don't forget old Melikos holds a Black Belt for judo and karate."

Then little kids round about had opened their ears and asked silly questions, so they'd had to stop their talk, but as Bill walked on now, he hoped Steve would do those equations quickly and catch up with him.

His thoughts came back to leaving the opal field. Leaving! He'd never lived anywhere else—not that he could remember, anyway. He had been here eight years, since he was five, and a lot longer than most of the men, who came and went. People asked him questions, even his advice—like they did the oldtimers—and accepted his answers. He knew as much about mining for opal as his father, and he could do most things connected with it. Leaving! And Grandma Birch's house wasn't big enough for Steve and Potch.

It was at that moment that Potch caught up with him. "Potch."

The dog lifted his head as he loped in close to Bill's heels. Usually he was waiting at the schoolroom door for the boy. But sometimes it took him a long time to make the journey from the dugout on Watson's Hill to the school door, depending on how many times he had to deviate to avoid one of his own kind.

The dog was thirsty, and his tongue was hanging out. But Bill knew he would not put that tongue under the drip from the waste pipe at the store. The other dogs of the town went there.

How could he leave Potch here? Yet Grandma Birch had said she wouldn't have a big dog in her house. She had made that quite clear—no big dogs and no Aborigines.

Yet how could he leave him? No one would tolerate him in the town because he was afraid of his own kind. For the rest of his days he would be hungry and thirsty. And he couldn't shoot him. You couldn't take life from someone you loved.

So Bill scuffed his feet, and the stones ground at his new thongs like sandpaper, taking bits out of the plastic, and even out of his hard coarsened toes.

Then he began to quicken his pace. He didn't want to miss Nikos—if he came.

As it happened, Mr. Robbins had asked Liz also to stay back this afternoon and finish a project under his direction. She worked at one end of the classroom while Steve and a couple of others worked at the other. But Steve finished his equations and disappeared homeward half an hour ahead of Liz.

Mr. Robbins was pleased with her work. She would do well, he said, at fourth-year high school next year. In fact, he was sure she would get a scholarship that would save her parents the cost of her fees. Not like that Bill, who would be lucky if he ever made high school. Mr. Robbins was very angry about Bill.

"He could do it if he wanted to!" he growled at Liz. "He's the laziest little scamp."

"Only with schoolwork," Liz defended him. "He can work as hard as Dad out at the mine."

"That's it! He's got this opal fever very young."

Sometimes Liz felt a bit guilty about her own ability to do schoolwork so easily, to study, to take delight in a project well done. Neither Mike nor May had gone beyond a proficiency certificate, though the latter had done a business college course and worked for a time as a typist in a city office. It was the office—and that German grandfather—that caused May at times to add a certain tone to her speech. Mike often pinched her on these occasions—which were mostly when an opal buyer called, or Mr. Robbins came to have a few words—and Liz, though she loved her, squirmed.

Now, as Liz set off over the squat hills, facing into the westerly and the dust—and hurrying because she hated both—she, too, thought about next year. Bill had told her briefly, at lunchtime, what had happened in the mines warden's office that morning; how that five-bedroom house in Glenelg had collapsed over their heads like the roof of a drive when an inexperienced miner removed a supporting pillar for its opal.

It was very depressing after the rosy excitement of last night, especially as she couldn't forget the Greeks who had stood in line behind her outside the post-office window and listened to her conversation.

Next year . . . She wouldn't be altogether happy about leaving, and she was truly sorry that the way was so hard for Bill and her father. But she knew she wouldn't do anything to stop it or defer it. She knew which way she had to go. And that made her think of Kathy. She couldn't foresee the way ahead for Kathy.

Kathy had been very quiet today. She had chewed her pencil and stared outside at the hot sun. She appeared mesmerized by the drone of the westerly that had risen just as school started, blowing the red dust into evil scarecrow figures hastening constantly past the windows.

And when school finished, she had only waved as she went out to the Land Rover that waited to take the Aboriginal children out to the Reserve, where she would change her clothes. Usually she held up the departure of the vehicle while she said her last words to her friend, until William, the half-Afghan, half-Aboriginal driver, would shout, "Come along there, will yer? Ain't got all day!"

Liz didn't scuff her feet, but she walked with eyes squinting against the wind and dust, thinking . . . soon . . . soon . . . soon. . . . With her eyes focused only far enough ahead to keep her on the track, she wasn't prepared for the shout. "Liz! Liz!"

Kathy, followed by three dogs, was running across the flat, thin black legs and bare feet raising a separate willy-willy behind her. She was wearing her own dress now, a dress that had probably belonged to a grownup down south and which flapped around her, nearly to her ankles and as big as a tent.

George Murphy had paid the mission ten cents for it, and felt that as it covered so much of her, it was a good buy. Of course, as he openly regretted, he could have got away with a zac if his old woman hadn't said, loud enough for that mission fellow to hear, "Pay ten cent—that good."

"Liz!" Kathy was breathless by the time she reached Liz, and the dogs jumped around excitedly. She was smiling a greeting at her friend, the wide mouth showing the good strong white teeth, but there was not the usual smiling light in the dark eyes.

"Liz—they took Ruthie today!"

"Took Ruthie! Who?" Liz put down her briefcase of books, turning her back to the wind, while the dogs milled around. "What are you saying, Kathy?"

"They came an' took her—said her belly was too big an' her legs too thin, an' she ain't had enough to eat!"

"Who took her?"

"Welfare officer—that woman."

"Oh-h-h . . ." Liz understood. All the dark people of the flat referred to "that woman"—the social welfare officer who regularly appeared in their territory and took, to their mind, an entirely unnecessary interest in the amount of fat on their children's legs and the size of their bellies.

"She took Ruthie . . ." Kathy's eyes were large and sad.

"Ruthie was sick?" Liz prompted.

"No. Just her belly an' her legs."

"But she cried a lot, didn't she?" Liz persisted. "You've told me how Margaret has asked you to mind her, often, because she cried so much."

"Yes," Kathy admitted.

"Taken her to the hospital, have they?"

"Yes. And they're not going to give her back to Margaret any more—says she doesn't look after her."

"That's about true," Liz said soberly, thinking of Margaret sitting in the dust of the galvanized iron hall the day the tourists had looked at them. "That sister of yours—and her no-good husband—are nearly always drunk, Kathy."

Kathy stood straight and looked directly at her friend. She knew the answer. She had heard the grownups give it many times. "An' who taught her to drink?" she demanded. "White fellow miner! Him—you know him."

Yes, Liz knew him. No one man in particular. The miners drank a lot themselves, doing such thirsty work in that thirsty land. It was their own scourge, as well as that of the

Aborigines. It robbed many a man of the fortune he dug at such great cost and effort from the ground, and of his dignity. Liz was old enough to be thankful that neither Mike nor Carl was troubled this way. But she couldn't deny Kathy's accusation.

"This'll be good for Ruthie," Liz said.

Kathy began to cry then. "Reckoned you'd be sorry, Liz. Reckoned you'd tell me how to get her back."

"I am sorry." Liz put her arm around the girl's shoulders, feeling how thin she was beneath that tent. "But it's best for Ruthie. Sister Joan will feed her properly at the hospital, and her legs will grow strong enough to walk. She should be walking, Kathy. She's nearly two."

Kathy sniffed back her tears. "Margaret says Bull'll fight 'em when he comes home. He won't let them take his kid."

"He won't be out of jail for another six months," Liz said. "He's just gone in—for hitting the policeman. Ruthie'll most likely be in a Home by then—because this is the third time she's had to be taken to the hospital."

"You don't say good things." Kathy shook her head, pushing a dog aside with her foot. "I thought you would be sorry. But you don't care—you're going away."

"That's not true—I do care. It's just that I *know* this will be good for Ruthie."

Kathy stood silently then, just looking at Liz with those dark soft eyes, though Liz could see there was something else she wanted to say. At last it came out. "I won't be at school for a few days."

"Not at school—why?"

"My mob's going walkabout."

Liz frowned. "Where? What field?"

"Not to any field." Kathy sifted the dust with her black toes.

"Then where? There's nowhere around here for them to go for a few days. When your mob go from here they generally head north—or to the west coast."

"Not always. Sometimes they got business round about." She obviously knew what the business was, and that it was important. Liz thought she seemed a little excited.

"Not something to do with Ruthie?" she questioned. It wouldn't be the first time that they had gone en masse to the hospital and demanded a patient.

"No." Kathy was definite. "Different kind of business. I tell you, later."

"All right. I hope it'll be something I want to hear."

"You don't always tell me things that I want to hear," Kathy said. "Me—I only tell you I go away for a few days. You say you go forever. What am I going to do, Liz?"

No matter what they talked about, it always came back to this. "What am I going to do, Liz?"

And because Liz was not yet sixteen, struggling with her own problems, she couldn't answer the dark girl's cry. She could only be sad, and wonder why, when you saw your course ahead, you had to take it—even though it made you sad. But perhaps, as Mr. Robbins said, you should be thankful that you could see the way ahead. And not be like Kathy, who could not see and for whom, on the opal field, there was no way to go but the way Margaret had gone.

As she turned again into the wind, Liz found that the westerly had strengthened, and now she had to force her way.

9

Judo and Karate

BILL did not really expect Nikos to be waiting at the site of the old bulldozer cutting to the left of the flat. He didn't really expect Nikos ever to wait again. He had done his job—tricked his friends into giving away the fact that Mike and Carl were on to a good thing, good enough for old Melikos to go to such lengths as stealing the compressor and emptying the petrol tank so that they would be late at the mines warden's office. (Bill didn't doubt for a moment now that these two thefts were by one and the same person.)

But one thing puzzled him. How had he and Steve—or he alone, perhaps—given Nikos the idea that Eldorado was good? They had realized how important it was to keep good fortune quiet—and they *had* kept it quiet. In any case, until yesterday, there had been nothing to give away, surely!

Bill sighed. Nikos had been clever—far cleverer than he and Steve. They had believed he wanted to be friends, wanted to get to know Australian boys, wanted to do things the way Australian boys did things, to learn, like them, to be independent at an early age. Nikos had said how hard it was to stand by and watch such freedom as Bill and Steve enjoyed. With a face a bit red, Bill remembered how satisfying it had been to be told these things, and how he had defended Nikos against the suspicions of his father and Carl.

But this was the kind of sabotage that was as mean and nasty as kicking a man on the ground. This betrayal of friendship hurt almost as much as the effects of the deed, allied to the fact that Nikos had been pulling his leg. Pulling his leg! He could hardly believe it.

Any more than he could believe his eyes when he saw Nikos sitting on the bank of the bulldozer cut, carelessly aiming stones across the chasm to the opposite side.

Bill almost turned and ran. Not because he was afraid of Nikos, but because of the confusion and anger in his mind and not knowing how to greet the Greek boy. He would have to beat him up, of course. No one let this kind of thing pass without proper notice. But did you just hop into him—after all, he would know what it was all about— or did you tap him first on the shoulder and say "Hi"?

The bulldozer cutting was a deep, wide scoop out of the earth's surface, more than a hundred feet long, twenty feet wide and fifteen feet deep, with the dump piled up like a ramp at either end. Bill always admired a bulldozer driver at work. The big blades ripped through the age-old rock and the six-foot-wide blunt-nosed shovel pushed it forward to the top of the dump. Often the machine was at a forty-five-degree angle, while the driver had to time his fall of rock with precision so that he didn't topple himself and the vehicle over his man-made hill. When they were down near the opal level, his mate walked behind, eyes sharp for the first glint of the precious gem.

But this way of winning opal was only for the man with a large amount of capital. A bulldozer such as this could cost twenty thousand dollars.

This was an old cutting, fallen in in parts, with desert swallows' nests in some of the shallow drives in the sides. Bill knew that thousands of dollars' worth of opal had been taken out of here, yet not a hint of that excitement remained.

It was peaceful here despite the wind, for although the area round about was pitted with craters, each ringed with stone of its own particular color, there was no shaft being worked within half a mile. Over by the shallow creek bed which flashed water only after a thunderstorm, someone was letting off gelignite—boom, boom, boom—a dull reverberating ball of sound. Automatically, Bill counted the shots—only half a dozen. Must be new chums enlarging a drive.

The desert swallows, with white topknots and breasts, were flying above the cutting, zooming, twittering, tossed by the wind. Brown butterflies, disturbed by that same wind, fluttered as low as possible, and Bill frightened many a lizard as he came noiselessly over the stones until he was only a foot or two from Nikos. Then he stopped.

"Well?" he demanded aggressively.

Nikos turned quickly, smiling a greeting. "Didn't hear you come," he said. "You can be as silent as an Aborigine."

"Not bad yourself—especially at night!" Bill said, noting that Potch had gone forward to greet the Greek boy.

That was why he hadn't barked in the night. As a rule, he was a good watchdog, but he knew Nikos.

Bill's bottom lip twitched when Nikos stroked the dog.

"Leave Potch alone!"

"Why?"

"He doesn't want to be stroked by you."

"He does. He likes me."

"Then he doesn't know you."

"He does. Look at him."

"You look at this, Nikos Melikos. Look at this!"

Bill thrust out the stone fan shell.

Nikos looked at Bill's dirty fingers, then bent forward eagerly and took the shell from him. "That's mine! Where'd you get it?"

"Where d'ye suppose?"

"I don't know. I didn't even know I'd lost it. But it's mine all right—got that chip out of the top."

"Yes. It's yours. An' I reckon you know where I found it."

"I haven't any idea. But I'm glad it isn't lost. That's my lucky fan shell—you said so yourself." Nikos put the shell into his pocket and stooped again to stroke Potch, but Bill thought the brown hand was trembling a little, and so it should.

"I'm going to beat you up, Nikos," he said, and decided that if an olive skin could whiten, Nikos's face whitened.

"What's the matter with you?" Nikos said roughly, and stopped stroking Potch to face Bill.

Bill wished then that he was not four inches taller than the Greek boy and that Nikos didn't have such a round baby face. He hated hitting anyone smaller than himself, but he was going to hit Nikos—going to hit him, mainly,

for making a sucker out of him. A city-slicker—a Greek
city-slicker—had made a sucker out of him.

They eyed each other for a moment. "I'm going to beat
you up," Bill warned again, but Nikos continued to stare,
unbelieving. Then Bill lunged.

It was a hard, smashing blow and with the impact Bill
felt the Greek boy reel backward toward the edge of the
cutting. For a moment he thought he was going straight
over but somehow Nikos, with extraordinary control of his
muscles, managed to right himself and came back in a half-
crouched attitude of defense.

Bill's eyes puckered up, burying the good nature that
usually shone there. He was going to make Nikos use all
the defense he knew.

They faced each other. There was an indrawn look to
Nikos's dark eyes—the left of which was not as wide-open
as the right—and a tenseness in his crouched figure as
though coiled for a spring.

Bill's fists were at the ready and after that first single second of summing up his right shot forward again.

But there was no connection this time. Somehow Nikos
came in close under that smashing right and his own right
arm shot like a tentacle around Bill's back, clamping fast,
while his left hand grasped the left sleeve of Bill's shirt.
The next instant Bill's feet had left the ground as he was
thrust in a quick somersault over Nikos's slightly-turned
right hip and landed on his back. He landed heavily because he hadn't absorbed enough of Nikos's judo teaching
to remember that his hands, not his body, must always
take the first shock of a fall.

But he was up at once, smarting under the whip of surprise, and took a spring at the Greek boy, carrying all his

weight with him. They tumbled and rolled then, not fighting the way Bill knew, blow for blow, but the way Nikos knew—the judo way.

Bill was so taken aback that all he could do was thump blindly when he could, and wriggle and squirm to extricate himself from one viselike hold after the other. And Nikos was never where he expected him to be. Just as he thought he had a grip the boy would slither away and come back at him with a hold from the rear.

Nikos was not younger, but he was shorter and plumper, with very smooth skin. He seemed to slide out of Bill's would-be grips as though he were greased.

And all the while Potch barked joyfully over their writhing bodies. He thought they were having a game, as they often did—the judo game that Nikos had been teaching Bill. Potch was always quick to defend against a human enemy, but then, of course, Nikos was not an enemy so he cavorted and jumped and barked, enjoying the game. When their heads were close together on the ground he tried to lick them between barks, and when they balanced precariously on the edge of the cutting, he barked an excited warning.

They fell in the end, just as Steve arrived. The red topsoil of the embankment gave way and they rolled down the rocky slope, flinging apart as they rolled—fifteen feet down.

It was a lucky fall for Bill. Nikos had just applied a strangle grasp to his head and what with blinding lights in his eyes and the tightening on his windpipe he was glad to fall and get away from Nikos. He lay for a moment or two at the bottom, aware of defeat—aware that he hadn't beaten up Nikos, who was so much smaller. It had been the other way round, and he had never felt so humiliated in his life. And there on top of the bank Steve and Potch were looking down at him. Potch had stopped barking but he was still waving that long thin tail.

Steve was grinning, his eyes twinkling. Bill looked funny down there, staring up at him with astonished eyes, still lying on his back, his head lower than his feet because he had ended up that way on the slope. Nikos had curled up as he fell and lay like an outsize bindy-eye burr a dozen feet from Bill.

"Hurt?" Steve shouted, and he and Potch looked down on their friends.

"No!" lied Bill, conscious that he was bruised from head to foot, but pride forbidding him to say so.

Nikos didn't answer but unwound himself and got to his feet. He brushed at the dust on his shirt and shorts and then began to walk away, toward the end of the cutting.

Bill was immediately made more furious. Nikos was treating him with contempt! Not even interested in carrying on the fight.

He ran after him. He flung a hand on his shoulder and spun him round, then gripped both shoulders. Nikos faced him, very still and quiet, dark eyes close.

"Oh!" Bill couldn't help the exclamation. Nikos's cheeks were wet, the dark of the eyes was hidden by welling tears. If Bill's first blow had connected, the tears hid the evidence.

Bill dropped his hands. Crying, eh? Like a kid. Perhaps the fall had hurt him, though there was no sign of blood. They looked at each other for a moment, then Nikos turned again toward the opposite end of the cutting, but he didn't walk as though he was hurt or bruised.

Bill watched him with angry, frustrated eyes. He couldn't fight a fellow who cried, not even the treacherous Nikos. Yet he felt no lifting of the sense of defeat as he watched the boy go. Blubberer or not, Nikos had had the upper hand in that fight. He had been beating Bill. And Bill knew that never again would Nikos wait at the edge of this bulldozer cut for him to appear after school.

It was not until the Greek boy had climbed the short slope out of the cutting and disappeared among the colored mounds of sandstone that Bill remembered that the petrified fan shell was now in Nikos's own pocket.

10

Dangerous Ideas

As IT happened, Bill and Steve arrived home from the encounter with Nikos just as Carl and Mike returned from the mine. All day Bill had been dreading this meeting with his father, not because of fear of punishment in the ordinary sense but because his father would believe he had betrayed him.

With Steve's help, he had cleaned the dust from his clothes and, by practicing all the way home, was managing to walk without a limp, despite a leg muscle that felt as though it had come unhinged and a number of bruises that would, normally, have earned him considerable solicitude but which, under the circumstances, had to be referred to as "dirty marks that won't come off."

The two boys had decided, tacitly, that there was no point in recounting the story of the beating-up of Nikos, which had proved to be no beating-up at all. Telling would confirm their own guilt, and even Bill was afraid of what his father might do if he knew about the stone fan shell.

For while May had a German grandfather, Mike had an Irish one and sometimes the Irish blood was quick to rise. It was no good denying either that sometimes violent deeds were done on the opal fields. And Mike's Australian-Irishness might prove combustible material when matched by Melikos of the Black Belt.

"Well, you've done it! You couple of young twirps!" Mike greeted them bitterly as he climbed from the utility. "And—goodness—we warned you enough!"

"You're sure it was Melikos?" Bill queried. Not because he had any doubts himself, but because he had to say something.

"I'm not sure of anything! Except that there is a Greek claim on all sides of us!"

"We don't know how we gave it away," Bill said miserably. "We thought we were careful enough."

"It'll be a long time before you're trusted with anything again, Bill," his father said. "A long time."

"You either, Steve!" snapped Carl. "You've not been very smart."

Bill hunched his shoulders then and started to drift down the slope away from the vehicle and the dugout. This hurt, and more than ever he couldn't tell his father about the fan shell, especially as he had let this evidence escape so easily. Never before had anything upset the close tie of mateship between him and his father. He kicked at a stone. Liz had a lot to answer for! If their father had not been under this strain to find a parcel quickly, he would have shrugged off this setback and given Bill the benefit of the doubt. Bill hated Liz and her learning, her nose always in a book, and the way she talked down to him as though she was already a grownup and a teacher.

Steve followed him silently. They were like two puppies disowned by the pack.

The days that followed were not happy ones in the Watson dugout. Each morning Mike, with Carl beside him, roared the utility down the ramp and thrust the vehicle over the stony road as though pursued by a devil, and each evening, or late afternoon, they returned. Strangely enough, the days on which they returned with gemstones in the calico bags May supplied were the days they returned with longer faces than they had gone out with. For the trace was leading them, inexorably and still horizontally, toward the northern outer edge of their claim.

And on this north boundary—in fact, on all boundaries—other men were now working. Eldorado was pegged in. And how many times had it been known that the claim next door—the one pegged after the first strike—was the one wherein the fortune lay!

Three of these men, at least, were new to the field, new to opal-digging and new to the Australian tongue. So that as Mike and Carl walked between the dumps that were rising rapidly around them, they didn't stop even to speak, or at least Mike didn't. Carl, who didn't have a family to consider and with a few more years left to dig for opal than Mike, was not quite so taciturn. He would nod his head to the impassive faces bent over the buckets.

On most nights they brought home some opal. It was of good quality and enough to make them quite certain that their trace was leading them to the parcel about which Mike had had a hunch.

But whether it would lie on their side of the dividing line or in the claim on the north side only hard work would reveal.

The work was hard indeed. Down seventy feet, without the aid of a compressor-driven jackhammer and with only a two-man team, progress was tediously slow and painful. Painful because, following the rumble of gelignite on all four sides, Mike and Carl knew that while they sweated with pick and shovel and cold chisel their rivals were vibrating to jackhammers. It was agony to know that these other men were better equipped to reach the fortune first.

Yet they were making more than just tucker money, and ordinarily Mike would have been pleased that they were at least getting wages for their labor, which was more than they had done for some time. But faced with the possibility of that parcel being snatched just ahead of him, he grew savage and remote.

May was thankful for the reward they were winning. It would be very useful when they went to town, and she helped to conserve it by being frugal with household spending. But she did not dare mention the impending move or hairdos, for even the sight of Liz studying deepened Mike's frown. Liz took to studying entirely in her bedroom, May put away the sewing that shouted "town," and Bill and Steve and Potch kept out of the way.

Toward the end of the week Mike announced that they couldn't wait any longer for a compressor-on-hire to be available, that they were going to sell the opal they had won over the last few days and buy a new one.

"Don't do that, Mike!" May begged. "At least let's keep this nest egg. You'll be glad of a few dollars behind you when we get to Grandma Birch's."

"I'll be glad of a few dollars all right!" Mike said. "That's why we're going to buy this compressor. We're going to work fast. We're going to hit that boundary before the Greeks—and we'll argue afterward just where that boundary is!"

May opened her eyes wide. "You wouldn't—infiltrate!"

"Look here, May! We were tricked out of those other claims—the north one, anyway—the one that mattered. Now we're going to play them at their own game. We're going to follow that trace as far as it takes us, or until we meet those fellows coming the other way."

"You can't! Those men have got the law behind them. You wouldn't have a chance with the mines warden if you went beyond your boundary. You could end up in jail, Mike! You know you can't *prove* that the petrol was even stolen!"

"No, I can't prove it. And I'll admit that I can't even be sure it's Melikos. Those fellows working around us—three are new ones, and a couple have only been here this one season—don't seem to pay much attention to Melikos. But that's nothing to go on—this might be part of his plan to put me off the scent. Anyway, I don't have to know who the guilty party is. I believe that we were tricked out of that north claim—and naturally the men working that claim must be the guilty ones or in league with the guilty ones. So my conscience is clear. I'm going as far as the trace goes—until someone stops me!"

"You're mad, Mike!" May cried. "We've never had a spot of this kind of trouble since we've been here. You can't afford to have things go wrong now. Grandma Birch won't want you if you get into trouble."

"Forgot that I told you, May!" Mike said roughly. "Or you'll do what young Bill did—give the show away."

He flung out through the wire door then and she knew he was going to find Carl and they would go at once to ar-

range for the purchase and urgent delivery of a new compressor from Adelaide. She sat down at the polished Laminex table, her legs weak and a sick feeling in her stomach.

She hadn't realized how much this parcel meant to
Mike. Of course, she had always known he had the fever,
ever since they'd found the stone in her ring, but she
hadn't imagined that it would ever befuddle his sense of
right and wrong. And whichever way you looked at it—
particularly from the side of the law—this was wrong. He
would buy trouble when he bought the new compressor.

They had had many ups and downs in their years of
wandering, but they had been the kind of misfortunes that
could be shrugged off or laughed about later. But you
couldn't shrug off or laugh about anything that set you
foul of the law. May got up and put the kettle on. A cup
of tea perhaps would help her to think what she should do
next.

In his bedroom, Bill sat very still on his bed. Neither of his
parents had seen him go in there, neither of them had
known he was there. He had heard every word, and he
knew exactly what the risks were. Even if the law didn't
catch up with his father, old Melikos would.

Bill had never felt so miserable in his life. He didn't
know how he and Steve had given the information to
Nikos, he only knew that he had had the evidence—if that
fan shell could be called or even used as evidence—in his
hand, and he had let it go. That when he might have got
justice for his father, he hadn't been willing to admit that
it was his fault. Now if his father did anything that put
him into that stifling lockup, he would be to·blame.

So Bill, too, sat still and tried to think what he should

do next. If only he could think of a *plan*! Some way to win enough opal to make this move from the Opal Town at least bearable. But all he could think of was that this trouble would never have arisen if it hadn't been for Liz!

Later, when he heard his mother leave the dugout and heard the old car—with new gears—buzz into life, he knew she had left to collect mail and newspapers, and it was safe for him to come out. He decided to go at once in search of Steve. Between them they must think of some way out of this problem.

A short passageway connected Bill's room with the living room, and he had to pass Liz's doorway. The curtain was not drawn and, for no reason at all, he looked in as he passed. As usual, it was a very tidy room, with nothing out of place except some papers left on the desk her father had made for her. They were in a neat pile. But there was no exhibit of opal here because Liz didn't care about opal.

No, Liz only cared about her books and her lessons and her endless making of notes—nothing else. Those were notes piled so neatly on her desk. He couldn't read what was written from the doorway but guessed they were history notes. Liz had to work harder at history than the other subjects, and it helped her to paraphrase it all in notes.

The grownups, of course, thought the brains of the family might have been better distributed the other way round—even his father and Mr. Robbins, even May. Not that they expressed the thought quite like that. They just urged him to try to do better, told him he had ability of which he'd never dreamed. A boy had to earn a living to support a family, they said, a girl only for herself. Poor Bill, they said . . .

Suddenly he was across the tiny room and gathering up the papers into his hand. He looked at them for a moment. They were history all right—British history—written in that fine clear handwriting that Mr. Robbins was always praising. He thought, bitterly, that Mr. Robbins never praised *his* writing.

Suddenly he ripped the pages from side to side—zrsh . . . zrsh—and then from top to bottom—zrsh . . . zrsh . . . What a tearing sound, what an angry sound, what a sound of destruction! Zrsh . . . zrsh . . .

Bits of white paper with a delicate design in that fine writing fluttered around him. The whole floor seemed to be covered with bits of white paper.

Then he went cold. He had ripped Liz's notes—from side to side and from top to bottom! Torn up notes that were so important to her examination, that might make all the difference as to whether she passed or failed.

He looked at those remaining in his hand. With great clarity he saw that, in anger, he had done the first really bad thing in his life. Committed a cruel and spiteful act against another person—against his sister. He felt as though all the crimes that had ever been committed had been committed by him in this moment.

And childish, too. Childish as Nikos's crying. His face burned with the shame of it. He bent quickly to gather up the pieces and found it hard to get a grip on so many separate bits of paper.

Then he returned to his own room and wondered where he could hide this evidence. He would like to have burned it immediately, but there hadn't been a fire in the wood stove for a couple of months and wouldn't be again probably until next June or July, and he couldn't put the stuff into the incinerator, just in case his mother and Liz recognized the ash for what it was.

At last, he took a large biscuit tin containing specimens from his shelf and began to empty the tin. He would put the torn papers on the bottom. No one would ever look there and, later on, when Liz had stopped looking for the stuff and it was forgotten, he would take it out to an old shaft and burn it. He began to empty the tin of the pieces of jasper, two or three small clumps of petrified mud shells, a piece of rare "angel stone," dark and flinty, a stone periwinkle and pieces of opalized skin shells.

He was so intent that he didn't hear Liz come in. She walked quietly in her thongs, as he did, and she hadn't banged the wire door because she never did bang doors.

She saw at once the pile of paper waiting to go into the tin.

"Bill!" she cried out. "Those are my notes! What have you done?"

He turned, face scarlet, bottom lip thrust forward. To be caught disposing of the evidence doubled his guilt. "I—just did it. It's all your fault. Everything is your fault —because we have to go. Because of you!"

He flung past her, pushing her against the rock wall of the doorway, and the wire door screamed as he rushed out. Liz stood still for a moment, then began to pick up her history notes. It took a little while to gather up the pieces because her fingers trembled. She was not angry, only frightened. Frightened in the same way as she had been when her mother and father had rowed over their leaving. And accepting now that what Bill had said was true. It was all her fault.

Liz knew she would never tell her parents about the torn

history notes, because she never had told on Bill. In any case, what could she tell—that he had torn them because of her? Somehow that made her as guilty as he. So she just gathered them up and smoothed them and used nearly a roll of tape to fasten the pieces together again. She was thankful that each sheet had been torn only into four. Then she put them into a folder so that May wouldn't see and ask why they were torn.

She went to bed early that night, unable to study the long hours that were usually a pleasure rather than a chore. But sleep did not come easily. Her mind skipped from one to the other of those who would be most affected by the coming change. Bill, her parents, Steve, Kathy. Kathy! Strangely enough, it was Kathy she was thinking of when she at last fell asleep.

11

Ruthie

By THE time Kathy had been absent from school for four days, Mr. Robbins was very angry indeed. On the first day he had noted not only that the George Murphys were absent from the field but also that several other Aboriginal families had moved off the flat, and one from the Reserve. Inquiry revealed that all had left on that same morning, piling into their old cars and leaving very early, even before the earliest miner had set out for his diggings.

Mr. Robbins also noted that they were all from one particular tribe. He questioned some of the remaining Aborigines but they shrugged and said, "Know nothing, boss—they just up and go."

But he knew they knew. Worry and anger grew with each day, for he had his own ideas as to why they might have gone, but he didn't voice them to anyone, not even to Liz, although he and Liz often discussed this disturbing disappearance. In between times, Mr. Robbins and the young policeman and the missioner scoured the country as far afield as possible, but with no result. Kathy and her people had vanished.

Mr. Robbins could only promise himself that there would be a stiff truancy summons for George Murphy when he finally brought back his family. He would learn that this head teacher took a very strong line when Aboriginal parents kept their children from school, especially children like Kathy. Somehow the adults had to be made to understand that, for the children's sakes, they *must* be educated the white man's way now that—with distances always growing less—they couldn't escape being part of the white man's world. So Mr. Robbins worried and waited.

Liz, too, worried, but she took some comfort from the fact that Kathy had said she would be back. So unless the elders had tricked the girl into going far away from the opal field—perhaps as a form of retaliation for taking Ruthie from them—Kathy would be back. Liz knew that Kathy would not deliberately lie to her.

And on this morning, three days after Bill's mutilation of her notes, when Liz woke up and went out to the bathroom shed, she saw that there was smoke coming once again from a fire at the side of the old caravan, around which people and dogs were milling. The George Murphys were back.

Liz hurried then, and went off to school five minutes ahead of Bill. This was partly because there was still strain between them. His first reaction to her silence regarding the torn notes had been a fierce "Why didn't you tell on me?" He seemed resentful that she had said nothing, as though it placed him under an obligation to her, and that resentment remained. She hurried, too, because she was eager to know the reason for the walkabout and Kathy had promised to tell. She had a feeling, also, that it might be something Kathy wouldn't want Bill to hear. Kathy often became silent when Bill was about, because he'd say, "Aw-w, go on—don't pull my leg." This was a pastime Kathy just didn't understand and her only defense was silence.

So Liz left five minutes ahead of her brother, expecting to see the dark girl sitting on the yellow oil drum at the first curl in the track before the school. Kathy would be wearing the blue cotton dress and, probably, the blue sweater—although the morning was hot—that were issued daily at the Reserve.

It was usual for the Land Rover with its canvas hood and sides to bring the girls in first, because they were less mischievous than the boys and could be expected to play happily in the playground while they waited for school to begin. Not that Kathy ever played. With her long legs swinging she always waited on the oil drum for Liz.

But this morning Kathy was not there.

Hurrying on to the school, Liz found that the rest of the children of the Murphy mob were in the schoolground, but not Kathy. So then she sought out Mr. Robbins.

"Kathy's in the hospital," he said bluntly. "They knocked her tooth out—one of those fine, strong white teeth—to make her a woman. And, maybe because tribal law isn't what it used to be—because it's diluted now with white men's ways and wine—her mouth is infected."

"But Mr. Robbins . . ." Liz was horrified.

"She'll be all right," he said, still very angry. "Sister Joan is not worried about her. But poor Kathy's got a very swollen face and a bad toothache. And a gap in her front teeth for life!"

"But why?"

"There's more tribal law left among these remnants than we credit," he said, "and somehow the fuss over Ruthie brought it to the surface. I think they wanted to show that the Aboriginal culture—and the Aboriginal ways—are still here, and that they still mean much to them."

"Kathy's mentioned the knocking-out-of-the-tooth ceremony once or twice," Liz said slowly, "but I didn't think it would ever happen to her."

Liz knew something of this ceremony. In some tribes, including Kathy's, the child approaching young womanhood was taken into the bush by the older women, one of whom performed the evulsion of the tooth. The instruments used were a small sharp-pointed stick and an equally sharp stone; the gum was cut quickly—or sometimes it was bitten by the operator—and then the tooth levered out.

Liz knew about this, but somehow being at school every day with Kathy, seeing her learn arithmetic and geography and spelling and assembling with all the other children to salute the flag on Monday morning, made her forget sometimes that Kathy was scarcely one generation removed from another loyalty and another law.

"I didn't think it would happen to her either—in this present day," said Mr. Robbins. "For one thing, I thought she was too eager to be like you, Liz—and you haven't a front tooth missing—to make no protest."

"Do you think . . ." Liz could hardly bring herself to say it, "that it's because . . . I'm going?"

"Might have something to do with it," he said, and

turned away then because it was time to instruct one of the little ones to ring the bell for assembly. So he didn't see Liz's eyes cloud.

When school was over for the day, Liz asked Steve to take her books home for her—because Bill was still unfriendly —and to tell her mother that she would be later than usual as she was going to visit Kathy. Then she set off down the slope from the tableland on which the school squatted like a hen fluffing over a large setting of chicks, both white and black, to walk the mile out to the hospital.

The hill sloped gently down to the cluster of buildings that comprised the surface part of the town. All the business activity was wedged into a few hundred yards—the two stores, the motel and the open-fronted sheds in which vehicle repairs, such as the gearbox on her mother's car, were carried out. On the next rise a couple of gaudy slogans, complete with Aboriginal motifs, announced "The Opal Cave," "Gems for Sale," "The Dugout for Opal." There the tourists cavorted and prided themselves on striking a good bargain with shrewd opal men.

Now at the side of the store two Aboriginal men were fighting. Placed carefully against the wall were two flagons of wine, hobnobbing while their owners fought. They were middle-aged full bloods; they wore no boots and their uncombed hair was covered with dust.

They fought with slow heaviness. When one fell down, the other took the opportunity to gather his wind again, but they were intent just the same on punishing each other.

Some of their own people, and the dogs, were sitting in the shade of the store wall. Sometimes they shouted to the men but mostly they took no notice.

Liz watched them as she walked past down the hill. She recognized them both, and knew they were initiated men who were versed in tribal law. She wondered what the fight was about, and saw that one was bleeding already from the nose. But even as she passed they stopped the contest, and their anger ceased with the putting down of their fists. Each picked up his flagon and together they continued down the slope. Each was satisfied, and with good will restored, they would hold no grudge—that was tribal law. It was a good law. There was much in tribal law that was good, so much that the whites could learn. But they didn't learn—they taught. Taught bad ways such as a taste for that cheap flagon of wine, and because of it Ruthie was in hospital.

Liz found herself wishing that it was because of Ruthie —and not because of her, Liz—that Kathy, in her turn, was in hospital.

The track left the activity of the town quickly behind and wound out flat and stony to the hospital. Liz walked a little to the side of the wheel grooves, her feet crunching down the brittle dead surface growth left by the last rain. She walked quickly, scarcely noticing the occupants of the few vehicles that passed her and quite unaware that more than one male head turned to look back at the neat figure going its way with such purpose.

The Opal Town hadn't long had the Flying Doctor Service and a hospital. The hospital was built against a rise that broke the force of the westerly winds. It was a low-slung weatherboard building, with a wide roof to catch rain when it fell, and was completely enclosed with a deep wired-in veranda.

A chain-wire fence encircled the acre of stony ground—

ruts and holes smoothed out to make it level and neat—
that was hospital territory. The entrance was through a
wire door onto the veranda, directly opposite the door of
the main building.

As Liz reached the cool veranda, this inner door stood
open, revealing the shining vinyl square tiles, in two tones
of gray, that covered the passage running the full length of
the building. The other end opened into the yard, another
stony stretch but relieved at the door by four square feet
of cactus rock garden which Sister Joan Brown, who had
been in charge of the hospital since its opening, had
started.

On one side of the passage, three doors opened into
three wards, each holding either two or three beds; on the
other side were the office, surgery, dispensary, two staff
bedrooms, living room and kitchen.

Liz hesitated at the main doorway. The whole building
was quiet, with no sound of voices. Then she heard a
scuffing noise like a soft broom on the polished vinyl tiles,
and a small black head appeared from around the door of
the living room, propelled forward by two black straight
sticks of arms, followed by a tiny body and legs. It was
Ruthie.

Liz stood very still, knowing how frightened Ruthie
could be of strangers. Not that Liz was a stranger to her.
Kathy often had the child with her, minding her for her
sister, but she might not recognize Liz in these different
surroundings.

The child was dressed in a pink cotton romper suit. She
looked like a small black, pink-bellied spider as she half-
pushed, half-crawled across the floor. Her fingers were extraordinarily long and flexible and the nails and palms, like

the soles of her upturned feet, were pink, while the streaks of rust through her dark hair were like a henna rinse from a hairdresser. Obviously she was going nowhere, but intent on going. She moved along the passage, weaving a course with the alternating pattern of the color. She was advancing toward Liz and presently the girl's feet were part of the pattern.

Instantly the child stopped, her lip puckered and she began to cry even before she raised her big, black, long-lashed eyes to Liz's face.

"Ruthie," Liz said, but Ruthie was already wailing too loudly to hear, and there was movement from the living room.

"Ruthie," called Sister Joan Brown soothingly.

And another voice, from one of the wards—a young voice, but protective and loving—"Ruthie, come in here. Here's where I be."

But Ruthie continued to look at Liz through the long curtain of lashes in between poking small bony fists into her eyes. Sister Joan came quickly, and then she saw Liz standing there.

"Why, Liz—don't tell me you made Ruthie cry?" She laughed.

"Yes—it was me," Liz admitted, admiring the Sister's neat white uniform. She certainly looked older than she did in the short pink dress and sandals she had worn to the picnic, but very capable and calm and good. "She took one look at my thongs and let out that first yell."

The Sister swept the child up into her arms. "She takes fright easily."

"She looks so different, so clean and sweet," Liz said.

"She's a pretty baby—though exactly half normal weight."

"Will she ever make it up?"

"Of course. I'm not letting her go from this hospital until there's enough fat on those legs to carry her!"

"Then she will be able to walk?"

"Yes—strength is all she needs. There's nothing wrong with her—at least, nothing that good food won't cure. That sister of Kathy's hasn't any idea of proper feeding."

"But how did the Aborigines get on when they didn't know our way of feeding?" Liz frowned.

"They did very well on what they had," Sister Joan said, "but now people like Margaret, who are neither tribal nor learned in our ways—our good ways, anyway—fall between the two stools."

"Couldn't you teach her?"

"I've tried, Liz. I wanted Margaret and some of the other young women to come here and learn something of baby care. But either they were too shy or they thought it would be too difficult. I couldn't persuade them. They have to *want* to do these things before you can help them."

Sister Joan looked hard at Liz, and the girl knew that the Sister was thinking of Kathy and the influence Liz had with the dark girl.

Liz asked then, "How is Kathy?"

"She's all right—though still sore. I'll keep her here until her mouth is quite healed. She'll be glad to see you, Liz— second door. She and Ruthie are our only patients at the moment—healthy climate this. Not even a miner suffering from a bucket on the head!"

Liz was grateful to the Sister for not saying any more, and she went with some diffidence down the polished passage and through the doorway marked Ward Two. It was a bright room, with the vinyl squares cream and pink.

Kathy was in the second bed. She was sitting up, leaning against a pile of white pillows and covered by a pink cotton bedspread. Liz stared. She had never seen Kathy in a bed and doubted she had ever been in one before, unless perhaps on some of the mission stations through which her mob had passed.

"Do you like it?" Liz asked. "The bed, I mean?"

Kathy pushed back against the pillows and started to grin, only to snap her lips shut. But Liz had seen the gap in the top front teeth—the right center.

"Yes," Kathy said in a muffled voice. "Pretty good."

"Does it hurt?"

"No—don't hurt." Kathy pulled the pink bedspread up to her chin and looked as though she was about to slide down under the bedclothes. Sometimes she did that at school when a visitor off the tourist coaches came to the school and smiled at her. She would smile back, then self-consciousness would take hold and sometimes she would slide right down under the desk. Even Mr. Robbins would have to offer some inducement to get her out.

"Why did you let them do it, Kathy?" Liz asked.

Kathy opened her dark eyes very wide above the swollen cheeks. She was plainly surprised at the question, and asked her own question.

"You still goin' away?"

"Yes," Liz answered in a low voice, not looking at the dark girl and feeling the contraction of misery in her stomach. To subdue it, she came back at Kathy. "Why did you let them do it?"

"Why not?" Kathy said. "Reckon it's the law."

"I thought you knew better!"

"Better'n what?" Kathy peeped at her, as Ruthie had done, through long drooping eyelashes.

"Oh . . . I don't know!" Liz didn't know. Bits about the law were often coming up. She had heard recently that a man had had sticks inserted in his arms by his tribal elders —not Kathy's tribe—for some misdemeanor. But on Sundays Kathy went to Sunday school at the mission church in the morning, and often in the afternoon she came to the Sunday school conducted by Sister Joan at the hospital. She seemed to like the Bible stories and always listened quietly, sh-shushing the smaller ones who made noises and interrupted. It was all very mixed-up, and Liz thought how mixed-up Kathy must be inside. She felt she should do something to unravel the tangle, and stood quietly waiting for inspiration. But Kathy herself turned from the problem, if indeed it was such to her.

"Sister makes nice things to eat," she said. "Jelly and ice cream. Ruthie likes ice cream. Sister let me feed her today. And, Liz, she can drink milk now out of a glass proper— never spill a drop. Good as Mrs. Jim's kid."

"Mrs. Jim" was the young wife of Mr. Jim Jones, a miner of two or three years' standing. She had astounded everyone by remaining in the town to have her baby boy at the hospital. Now everyone, including the Aborigines, watched its progress with absorbed interest.

"Liz . . ." Kathy let the bedspread slide again, revealing that she was wearing one of Sister's own cotton floral nightdresses. "Liz . . . don't Ruthie look nice in that pink thing—romper, Sister call it. Reckon she looks as nice as Mrs. Jim's kid."

"Yes," Liz agreed.

"I'm going to feed her again with her tea. I like doing it. And we're going to teach her to walk."

Kathy seldom talked so much, even without that swollen face, but somehow Liz didn't feel close to her friend.

Kathy was shutting her out—because she was leaving her behind.

"I'll have to go home now," she said. "Steve was taking my books home for me, but Mum won't expect me to be too late."

Kathy looked up. "Does Steve know—about my tooth?"

"Yes."

"D'ye think—he will like me without it?"

"I don't know," said Liz, and because she was upset added, "You should have thought of that before you let them do it."

12

"Liz Shouldn't Have Come!"

BILL and Steve hadn't expected to be allowed near Eldorado again, but as it turned out their services were required on the very next Saturday.

The new compressor was not expected to arrive by transport until Monday or even later in the coming week, and both Mike and Carl had been working with a certain frantic haste. Even Carl's philosophical acceptance of things seemed to have been disturbed, for on the Friday he not only forgot to take replenishment for their tin of fat but also worked without his usual methodical precision. He was using the big twenty-two-gallon drum to raise the dirt, and slinging the drum along the skid pole, whinging without its grease, required a certain finesse. In his eagerness to shift one particular load quickly, he took too much of the weight on his own back.

Today, he could neither bend nor sit in any comfort and was forced to abandon all thought of work.

When Steve brought the news, just as Mike himself rose

on that Saturday morning, Mike was disappointed enough
to swear, but not in German. May, with sausages spitting
in the frying pan, cautioned him. "You have to break that
habit, Mike. Don't forget, we'll soon be in town and
Grandma Birch doesn't . . ."

"Like profanity!" he yelled.

"You'll wake Liz!" May shouted back. "And she has to
study today. That exam's getting near."

"Carl said to take me," Steve said.

"Mm-m-m," Mike sighed. "Haven't got much choice,
have I? You and Bill it will have to be. I have to keep that
stuff moving somehow. Better make the tucker-bag heavy,
May. They eat like horses."

Both boys were happy to be part of the work force
again, even though the thought of working a stone's throw
from old Melikos of the Black Belt, and Nikos, was a little
disturbing. A Black Belt could have a very depressing
effect if you were not the wearer, Bill decided, but he
didn't say this to his father.

Breakfast over, they headed outside to the utility. It was
then that Liz came flying after them. She was dressed in a
cotton shirt and jeans, with an old cap on her yellow hair.
In each hand was a double slice of bread and butter and
Vegemite.

"My breakfast . . ." she panted. "Knew you wouldn't
wait while I ate anything else."

"What d'ye mean?" growled Bill.

"I'm going with you. I can give you boys a spell on the
winch. Or one of you can go down the shaft with Dad and
I'll help the other on top."

All three of them gaped at her as she climbed into the
cabin of the truck. "Come on—let's go," she urged, eyes

on the wire door. She wasn't sure just how long it would take her mother to recover from the shock of her announcement, but certainly not long. Not as long as it was taking the boys to close their mouths and to stop their eyes from popping.

"Come on, Dad," she cried. "Get in. I know you'll find me useful."

"Could be," Mike agreed vaguely. As he began to climb aboard, May banged out of the door.

"You can't take her!" she shouted. "She has study to do —and she'll ruin her hands!"

Mike was already letting out the clutch.

"It's ridiculous!" May cried. "Better for me to go than Liz!"

Mike swung the vehicle round onto the sloping track. "Won't do her any harm," he said, grinning for the first time that morning. "Do her good to see how the other half of the family lives."

May actually stamped her foot then, and Nancy, who had followed her out sedately, reeled aside. May never did such things. "Don't let her ruin her hands!" she pleaded.

As the truck crossed the flat, Mike asked his daughter, "What made you come, Liz?"

Liz said, "I heard what Steve said about Carl, and thought I could be useful. But I knew Mum would stop me if I gave her long enough to think about it." She was thankful that he didn't question her further.

She couldn't tell him that listening to Sister Joan yesterday and seeing Kathy in the hospital—coupled with Bill's attitude—had divested her study books of their savor.

In the back of the utility Bill and Steve and Potch were glum. Liz's presence at Eldorado would only be a hindrance and a liability.

Miners on the Greek Patch were working industriously, as the season for the year's mining was drawing to a close. Another month or six weeks would see the population of the Opal Town and the various outlying fields begin to dwindle. Not many men worked through the summer months when the temperature often stood for days at 120 degrees, with sun peak much higher, when there was not a single blade of green anywhere, when a wedgetail eagle would hang like a black kite in the sky and the dogs of the town would pant and droop and die for want of water.

Already the days were hot, keeping around the hundred-degree mark, and men were covering their usually bare backs with yellow-stained shirts and protecting their heads with some kind of hat. They mostly preferred to start work in the early dawn, pulling the stone for the first few hours —by which time the man on the winch was sweating down into his boots and the iron lever and the iron bucket were searing even to hardened skin. Then they would work underground until about midday. No wonder May called out, "Don't let her ruin her hands!" After all, in a few weeks those hands were to be introduced to Grandma Birch's neighbors.

Now as the Watson utility drew nearer Eldorado, Mike saw at once that the activity here had a different pattern than usual. For one thing, the winches on three of the flanking shafts—east, west and south—stood idle while several men were busy at the head of the north shaft. They were handling the up-coming bucket with speed and agility. Up and down, up and down. No words seemed to pass between them, but they worked with such concentrated energy that Mike was frowning as he drew his vehicle to a standstill. They had to leave the utility beyond the new south shaft because of the mound and the rubble that blocked their way.

"Something's going on," he muttered to Liz as he jumped from behind the wheel, with the two boys and Potch close behind.

They picked their way past the gaping shaft of the south claim, where the winch stood idle and the air sock hung like a white sausage.

The short, muscled men on the north claim appeared to pause momentarily to eye them and then to renew their efforts at greater speed.

"I don't like it," Mike said.

"Those men are new around here, aren't they?" Liz asked.

"Three of that team have been here only a few months."

"I saw them in the post office a few weeks ago," Liz said. "I thought they were new."

Mike looked across the rainbow of mounds to the right, to where Melikos was squatting, as he always seemed to be squatting, with pliers in hand and a coil of yellow fuse in front of him. As usual, he was preparing charges to let off when he took his lunch break. He was taking no notice of the group on the north claim, but Mike was undeceived.

"Thick as thieves!" he snarled. "If I had one scrap of evidence, I'd make that fellow eat it!"

Bill, just behind him, pursed his lips to whistle but didn't. It was not a whistling matter, even though it would have been interesting to see old Melikos digesting a petrified fan shell. Bill looked across to the Melikos camp from a corner of his eye, and thought that old Melikos could suddenly stride across the dumps and put an arm lock on Mike, calling on his henchmen to strangle-hold the rest of them. On Liz? Well, maybe. Greek women seldom figured anywhere but in the home and the kitchen, so perhaps they would even strangle-hold Liz because she was here, at the shaft, preparing to wind a bucket up from below. It might even be good for her. Shake some of that silly learning out of her head and replace it with those bubbling stars he had seen himself.

But unfortunately—with those fellows on the north claim as well—the Watson gang would be badly outnumbered.

So Bill was relieved—even though the relief shamed him—to see that Pappa Melikos did not take his interest from his fuse and his detonators, and that Nikos continued to wind the winch busily, as though the Watson group was invisible.

Then Bill mentally pinched himself. How stupid of him —of course they would give no sign. They were in the wrong, even if he had started the fight with Nikos. From this distance he couldn't see the state of Nikos's face, but he hoped he still carried trace of a black eye from that one and only blow he had managed to land home. Only one blow! It was galling to think about. He wished Steve hadn't seen his defeat.

"We'll get cracking," Mike said curtly. "There's a lot of stone to come up from yesterday. That should bring us to the boundary. You can come down with me, Bill, while Steve and Liz carry on up here."

It was Liz who lowered them down, first her father, then Bill. Bill was surprised at the way she went to work, as though she'd never read a book in her life, or knew a thing about British history. And she had firm muscles, too, in those smooth arms, not like some sissy girls. Grudgingly, he admired the way she lowered the sling, but he didn't pretend to understand why she had chosen to come with them. Funny things, girls.

Then he stepped onto the chair, curving his feet around the iron bar and clutching the steel cable. He liked the sway and turn of the cable as he went down. It reminded him of a dog-man he had seen, on that last visit to the city, being lowered by an enormous crane and revolving slowly above the teeming traffic.

Bill went down quickly, keeping himself clear from the rasping surface of those close white walls with his free hand and feeling the cool underground air coming up to meet him.

His father was already filling the bucket when he joined him, and he saw that there was a good deal of rock to be moved before the next set of charges could be put in.

The drive was at least sixty feet beyond the shaft now, with an extra air vent halfway, but with light from the generator it was a cool and well-lit tunnel. The globe seemed to pick up the gleam of the gypsum in the ceiling and give it a living sparkle. Carl and Mike had cut a good drive—high enough almost to walk upright and three feet wide. They must have worked hard indeed to have driven so far in such a short time.

But of course they were following trace, with a tiny pocket here and there to reward them, and men worked with a strange untiring energy when on trace, especially men who had once seen and found precious opal. Such as the opal in May's ring, the opal that had lashed Mike to a windlass handle ever since and would never let him go. Young as he was, Bill knew that. His father had the fever:

the opal fever. It lured men on and never let them go.
May should understand that.

As fast as Liz and Steve could lower a bucket, it was
filled with stone and pulled to the surface.

Mike didn't talk. He worked savagely.

It was Bill who said, "Listen, Dad—I can hear something."

Mike said, "Of course you can hear something—and it
isn't the boom of gelly!"

"Then you've been listening, too?"

"Of course I've been listening."

They both stood still. And the silence of their hole underground—seventy feet down and sixty feet in, where it
would have been blacker than night without that artificial
light, where there was nothing that lived or moved, not
even a spider, except themselves—wrapped around them
like a presence.

Except that somewhere beyond their hole, beyond their
rock walls, there was a sound. A faint rhythmic sound . . .
thud . . . thud . . . thud. They both knew what it was. A
pick at work. However, not one pick, but several picking
out a tune . . . thud . . . thud . . . thud. Gentle thuds,
muffled by the wall between, but real and unmistakable.

"They're nearer the boundary than we are!" Mike said
grimly.

Bill didn't question his father's statement. The miner
worked with a rule and compass. He knew to within inches
how far and in what direction he was driving, and he could
plot his figures on paper and show on the surface the plan
and scope of his workings from the main shaft. He had to
be able to do this so that rights could be definitely established and murder prevented.

Mike went on. "They must have worked night and day, in shifts, to get down so far in the time."

"Why would they be so sure which way to drive?" Bill said, miserable for his father and himself. "Dad, even if Steve and I did give away that you thought you were on to something, they couldn't be *sure* any more than you were."

"But I *was* sure—I *am* sure!" Mike blazed. "It's here. And somehow—they sensed it."

"But Steve and I didn't talk to *them*!"

"You talked to Nikos."

"But, Dad . . ."

"Get on with filling that bucket! We have to get through this rock . . . fast!"

Bill worked as a man would work, shoveling the dead-weight of stone into the bucket, wheeling it to the shaft, giving the signal that it was coming up and turning to fill the empty one behind him. Mike was picking now, with the same soft thud as that coming from the claim next door. Picking, picking, picking with the short-handled two-headed pick and bending now, lower and lower, to follow the trace.

The trace was mostly potch, but potch with the gleam of the rainbow colors. It varied constantly in width, from an inch to a fine thread, and sometimes from that fine thread flamed red fire. Precious opal. Just a thin line— almost too fine for the cutter's saw or the polisher's wheel. But nevertheless the precious gem. The gem that could be worth five hundred dollars an ounce!

With the sandstone rubble removed from close to the face, the seam was revealed bright and distinct, nearer the floor of the drive and on a more downward trend, but still running inexorably north into the north claim.

Mike was picking with great caution but as fast as his long experience would allow.

"It has to be in the next couple of feet!" he muttered, talking to himself and not Bill. "It *has* to be!"

He was gouging now beneath the seam, so that a gentle tap would release each stone from its jigsaw-puzzle shape into his waiting hand. He was burrowing a hole that was swallowing first his head, then his shoulders, then his body, until he was working on his stomach, with the electric-light globe at the entrance to this flat-roofed aperture. He removed each piece with infinite care. Not that this was the fortune. This was only the pointer. But they were valuable stones nevertheless, and must surely lead to the truly big pocket.

Now the seam had stopped veering down and was keeping that direct northern line. Only Mike's legs dangled from his envelope-like opening. Almost on his shoulders rested the weight of the earth—seventy feet of sandstone; almost his whole body was swallowed up in the flat cavern he had gouged.

Once the trace changed to a bright blue potch, an inch-thick band that looked like unblemished fine blue china.

Bill stood by watching until his father said, "Keep the bucket moving! We haven't found it yet—and old Melikos is watching."

Bill filled the bucket automatically, his eyes still on the part of his father's body that he could see. As often as he dared, he bent to look at that strong blue trace.

Then they heard it—the shout. The great wild shout that rumbled into them like the muffled roar of a fracture.

Mike gave a kick and a wriggle and slid out from the shelf, his face suddenly gray. "They've got it! Listen!

They've found the parcel—just on the other side of that two feet of sandstone that divides us!"

Bill didn't try to deny it. He knew it was true.

Mike listened. "It's a big parcel! Men don't roar like that unless it's a big parcel. They keep quiet—unless it's so big that it doesn't matter who knows!"

Bill didn't try to deny that, either. He knew it was true.

"In any case," Mike added, suddenly weary, "they know they can't drive any farther this way—so it doesn't matter who knows. They've got it, Bill—d'ye understand?—*my* parcel."

Bill nodded, though the movement was scarcely noticeable because he was standing back now from the glare of the electric light so that his father wouldn't notice his face. But he was looking at his father's face, and seeing the gray disappointment.

"Another day—and we'd have reached it ahead of them," Mike said, very quietly.

"You'd have been over your boundary . . ."

"Yes. I'd have been over my boundary. But that was *my* parcel, Bill—this shaft was *my* hunch." He gave a sudden crooked grin. "At least I've been saved from breaking the law!"

Then he began picking again because it was habit to use the tools rather than to stand staring at the sandstone face. But now the blue potch was narrowing to a barely discernible line, though still running horizontally north. It was plain enough that this mere thread led to the pocket that had occasioned the shouts in the drive next door.

Suddenly Mike threw down his pick and stood upright. "Our work in this hole is finished. Don't bother to send up that bucket of rubble. Tip it out here, and go up yourself."

Bill did as he was told, then after giving the signal cord a pull, put his foot onto the chair, grasped the rope with one hand and carried the empty bucket with the other. He spiraled slowly upward, keeping himself clear of the white sandstone walls with an occasional push with his free hand.

Steve and Liz were peering at him from the top of the shaft as he gradually drew level and threw the bucket out onto the rubble with a frightening clatter.

"What's happened?" Liz's face was streaked with dirty sweat runs and, although she was wearing a hat, her eyes were screwed up against the glare of the strong sunlight on the dazzling white sandstone rubble that surrounded them like the high wall of a moat.

"Finished," Bill said. "Send the sling down—Dad's coming up."

As Bill jumped clear, Steve rapidly reversed action and the empty sling raced down.

"We heard shouting from the north claim," Liz said, "and over the last little while they haven't sent up any buckets of stone."

"No need. They've found it."

"You mean . . . ?"

"Judging by the row they were kicking up—yes."

None of the three spoke after that, but all stood staring across to the north claim. The winch was turning but it was men they were bringing up from below, not stone. Noisy excited men. Talking and laughing in their own tongue—calling words up and down the shaft to those still below. Behaving as men might be expected to do who have found a parcel, especially men who haven't been too long on the field and have just looked on the fiery colors of a fortune.

Mike didn't come up on the next turn of the winch but sent up his picks and shovel in the empty bucket. As the sling went down again, a couple of the still wildly excited men from the north claim left the shaft to go to their shabby utility that stood nearby. They passed within twenty feet of the two boys and girl, their bodies rippling with excitement and shining with sweat. They looked at Liz as they passed, and one of them, in between a flow of Greek, kept repeating a word—"hunch, hunch, hunch."

In the burning heat of the sun, Liz turned cold. That was the word she had used at the post office. Hunch!

She was glad they had passed before her father's dark head showed above the ground, and she stood by silently as he gave directions to the boys to collect their gear and stack it on the utility—the winch, the safety ladders, the generator. Mike was abandoning Eldorado completely. It was heavy gear to move but between them they managed to hoist it into the tray.

Bill tried to protest. Surely there was something they should do before walking away from this hole forever! A "monkey" perhaps . . . Sometimes a miner put down an exploratory hole, known as a "monkey," to the next level through the floor of the drive instead of working back from the main shaft, and sometimes it rewarded him.

"Dad . . . what about a monkey down to the next level?"

"No."

Bill pleaded. "The seam might hit a heavy band and double back."

Mike shook his head. "No. That was it. That trace scarcely wavered—north and horizontal. And that other company got it."

"But, Dad . . ."

"No argument. I want to get out, Bill, before I do some-thing your mother will be sorry about. I have to remember we're going to Grandma Birch's."

Bill looked across to the Melikos shaft, where the men from the north claim, still milling and shouting, had joined old Melikos, though he still managed to look sour. He was a good actor, Bill thought drearily.

"Couldn't we have a go at them, Dad?" he entreated, quite forgetting any earlier nervousness on this point, and waving a brown arm toward the group.

"Not with Liz with us. There would be only you, Steve and me, against how many? Eight or nine, at least. The re-sult wouldn't be a nice sight for Liz."

"Please don't fight," Liz said, feeling cold inside in spite of the perspiration flowing down her body.

"Aw—gee! We could lick 'em! And Liz needn't look."

"Maybe we could." Mike managed a grin. "But we could also end up in the lockup with bandaged heads."

"I knew Liz shouldn't have come!"

"Don't blame her!" Mike said sharply. "I don't fancy that lockup. Which goes to show, boy, that I have indeed reached the years of discretion. And when that happens it's time—as your mother says—to leave the field." That was a statement without a grin, and Bill saw that it was useless to say any more.

He hated his sister and wished now that he didn't have to squeeze in beside her in the cabin, but the tray was piled high and there was no room there for passengers, not even for Potch.

As the vehicle swung away from the Greek Patch, Bill felt ashamed. Ashamed for himself and for his father. To just pack up and go and leave them to it. Leave them with all that opal that had been his father's hunch.

He looked across and saw that the Melikos winch had stopped working and that all had gathered in a little huddle, bending over something spread on the ground. The parcel! They were so intent that they had lost interest even in the passing utility.

Bill felt sick, and was surprised when he looked at his sister to see that she looked as he felt. Steve was quiet, too. Not because they had missed the parcel, as such, but he was sad because Bill was sad.

And Potch, who reacted like a harp string to Bill's mood, pressed close to the boy's legs and loved him.

If for nothing else, Bill blamed Liz for this quick retreat, this ignominious retreat. If she hadn't been with them, there would have been no silly talk of "years of discretion." They would have hopped into old Melikos and all the rest. He had known it was bad to have Liz go along with them.

13

A Plan at Last!

IT WAS long past lunchtime when they reached the Watson dugout and they had not eaten since leaving home. Mike had barely spoken on the journey. After ramming on the brakes, he was out of the utility immediately, heading toward Carl's dugout, though it wasn't good news he was taking to his friend. The young people followed more slowly. In a moment their mother would appear and it would be their misfortune to tell her what had happened.

But despite their noisy arrival, May did not appear and then they noticed that the blue car was missing. May had evidently gone to have lunch with Mrs. Jim, who was her particular friend.

Liz led the way, carrying the tucker-bag into the cool dim dugout.

"I'll make a cup of tea to eat with our sandwiches," she said. "Might as well have a cup of tea."

"Don't know how you can think of eating!" snarled Bill, already opening the bag.

136

"I'm not hungry," Liz said, filling the kettle from the sink tap and noting how the steel sink was shining. Her mother loved to see her possessions shine, which was another reason why she was looking forward to the city life. Liz knew she would be glad to leave the dust that was often thick as a fog, drifting in wherever there was an entry, wrapping itself around every object.

The boys sat at the table, spreading the sandwiches on the Laminex top. Both started to munch steadily, while Potch slipped in underneath and lay at Bill's feet. He took no notice of Nancy, who bared her upper teeth as he settled near her.

Liz stood by the stove, leaning on the sink, waiting for the kettle to boil and not caring whether they ate all the food. Her throat was tight, and she doubted that bread and salami sandwiches would find room to go down. Hunch! Hunch! The word was an imprisoned moth in her brain, going round and around and around.

Those men—those men who had been latecomers to this opal season—had looked at her and laughed and cried out hunch, hunch. Her father's hunch!

She didn't doubt what it meant. They had been new to the town—most of them, anyway—new to opal mining, and looking for a lead. New enough to the field to be ready to seize any directive—even if Bill and her father did seem to think that they were in league with Melikos; new enough to take the advice of anyone who said, "Dig under that saltbush—just as likely to be there as anywhere else"; and they had caught at her careless words.

It was all her fault.

What a cold, dead sensation it was to know that you were to blame for disaster that struck at those you loved.

Or did she love them? Did you really love people when you were willing to sacrifice them to your wants? Perhaps she wasn't really capable of love! The thought chilled her —not to be capable of love. It was too much to bear. Not only was she to blame for their prospective leaving of the opal field, but also for the loss of the parcel that would never come their way again. For it was a big parcel, that was certain, and a miner seldom had a second chance at a truly big parcel.

Liz slumped her shoulders. What a dead, cold feeling it was.

She didn't realize that the kettle was boiling until steam lifted the lid and water bubbled over the clean stove. She made the tea and took it through the stone archway to the living room, while the boys watched her with cold eyes.

"You shouldn't have come with us," Bill said flatly. "We could have had a lash at them if you hadn't been there."

"I'm glad you didn't have a lash at them." Liz sipped her tea, finding it tasteless. "It wouldn't have done any good."

"We've never been as near to a good thing," Bill said bitterly. "Never will be again."

"Wish it wasn't our fault." Steve sighed. "We should have seen what Nikos was up to, Bill."

Suddenly Liz found her guilt unbearable. She pushed her hair out of her eyes.

"I gave them the real clue," she said miserably. "I was talking to Maria at the store when she was giving out the mail—those men heard me."

She told the story then of what she had said. "And it was after that that the compressor was stolen—and the petrol—and the newcomers made those claims."

Bill's eyes remained as stony as the rubble in any dump. That she had confessed voluntarily had no softening effect on him. Her words only completed her blame in his eyes. "And you let Dad think it was us entirely—Steve and me."

"Bill, I only realized it today, when I heard the word those men used . . ."

"Well, anyway—it makes three of us," he said drily. "Only you're far worse than me and Steve, because it's your fault that we're going—and that's the root of the whole trouble."

"Yes," Liz agreed, and put down her sandwich. She couldn't eat anything, though Bill and Steve and Potch ate steadily, with no further word for her.

At last she said desperately, "We should do something!"

She said it mainly to break this accusing silence, not because she really thought there was anything she could do— except fail her exams. She had just decided that she must do that. And then repeat the year's work here, in the Opal Town. This decision would give her father another year. It was the least she could do for him, but her mother must never know. It would be very disappointing for her mother who, without doubt, had had her fill of adventure and was ready to be a suburban housewife with a teen-age daughter. But Liz felt that the year's gain for her father would more than balance the year's loss for her mother. "I'll do anything!" she offered.

"Anything?" Bill appraised her. "Anything we plan?"

"Yes. Anything."

"Well-l, Steve and I have a plan. We've been waiting for an idea for some time—and we reckon this is it."

Liz knew at once that it would be the bindy-eye, but she said, "Go on—tell me."

"We're going to put down that monkey in Eldorado—like I said to Dad."

"Oh-h . . ." Liz tried not to sound apprehensive.

"There could be opal on the next level."

"But Dad is certain there isn't."

"No one can be sure of anything where opal is concerned."

"I know."

"And we could do with your help on the winch."

She eased a little on her chair. At least he hadn't said that she would have to go down the shaft. "But when would you work it?"

"Tomorrow—Sunday."

"How? How are you going to get out there?"

"Well, I've just got a new tire on my bike, haven't I? I could dink you on the bar, and we'll borrow Old Welhelm's bike for Steve."

Liz hated the idea of being dinked nine miles over stones, but having confessed her guilt and said she was willing to do anything, she had left herself no escape. She was in Bill's hands.

"We have to start work straightaway," he said. "If the claim is left unworked for three days, anyone is entitled to jump it. And then we wouldn't get the chance to put down the monkey."

"But Dad brought home the winch and the motor—everything."

"There's an old windlass out there—left on an abandoned claim. We'll use that."

"It could be unsafe."

"Look here, Liz, can you think up any more objections? Do you want to help or don't you?"

"You know I do."

"Then stop moaning while we make our plans."

Liz sat very still, aware that in the last few minutes she had made two decisions that would alter the course of her life. One—to fail the exam; two—to remain here in the Opal Town for another year. And that could mean forever. Because she knew she would never be able to work as hard as she had worked this year—never perhaps reach this peak of learning again.

"We'll have to tell Mum and Dad a few white lies," Bill said. "Tell 'em we're going to visit Old Welhelm for the day. Pick up his bike and get out to the field in time to put in a few charges before midday. In the afternoon, we'll move what stone we can, and then—looks as though we wag it on Monday, Liz."

"Wag it . . ."

"Never get far enough down tomorrow to know what the level offers. Of course you'll miss a few lessons."

"It doesn't matter," she said quietly.

"Tools will be a problem . . ."

"We can gather a few old things together this afternoon," Steve said, "and hump them out past Welhelm's place, ready to pick up tomorrow after we leave the old fellow."

"We'll need gelignite, too . . ." Bill was still frowning. "I'll have to pinch a few sticks from Dad. Reckon I'll go out to the ute now and help myself before he comes back from Carl's and puts it all away."

"Just watch what you're doing, Bill," Liz warned.

"No schoolmarmishness, thanks. You're in this up to your neck, don't forget."

The two boys left her then with the dirty cups to wash and the remnants of the lunch to put away.

Liz wasn't feeling very cheerful. She had committed herself to Bill and Steve, but she hoped they would remember that there were certain aspects of opal mining that turned her cold—like crawling in confined spaces and feeling the pressure of the earth above. But she knew Bill was in the kind of mood in which he might not want to remember these things.

And May was going to be upset—having to wait another year for those roses and hairdos. Liz hated hurting her mother, who was more like a mate, and she could only hope that the easing of the tension which the delay in departure would bring would make up to her for that delay. It was sad that someone had to lose out, whichever course they took. And she thought, surely there should be—must be—a formula or a law, somewhere, that what blessed one must bless all; otherwise, life was always going to be unfair.

That made her think of Kathy. The change of plan might benefit Kathy, for another year would take her further on to maturity and a better grasp of better living. Perhaps it would help Kathy if she gave her a hint now that she might not be leaving the Opal Town at the end of the year.

By the time the cups were washed she had made up her mind to visit her friend. Quickly she went to her bedroom and changed the work-stained jeans for a clean cotton shift.

The boys were still making unobtrusive removals from the utility when she left the dugout. Bill eyed her.

"Where're you going?"

"To visit Kathy."

"What a good idea! As soon as we've hidden what we need for tomorrow, we'll visit her, too. That'll give us an alibi for this afternoon, at least."

Liz stood for a moment watching them pack up the box of gelignite and the box of detonators, with some paper under the top layer so that Mike wouldn't notice, at a glance, that any had been removed. It was unlikely that he would be letting off any more charges until he and Carl had selected another place in which to sink a shaft, so that their removal probably would not be missed for a few days anyway.

She waited until they had selected some picks and a couple of shovels from an old collection behind the laundry shed, saw them put the gelignite in a canvas bag carried on Steve's back and the detonators into Bill's pocket. At least they were taking precautions. Gelignite and detonators, she knew, must always be kept separated in case unexpected friction caused an explosion.

Although she had lived with gelignite for eight years, she still had a very real respect for the candle-length sticks that looked as innocent as pink lolly-sticks. She remembered that a year ago two youths had been skylarking with the explosive in a dugout on the other side of Watson's Hill and blown part of the dugout and one boy's arm to pulp. But at least she knew that, whatever his faults and his youth, Bill was a man of experience on the field.

Liz stayed until they started on their way around Watson's Hill in the direction of Welhelm's dugout shelter. She felt thankful that they hadn't asked her to go along and help carry the picks, which would be heavy by the time they reached Welhelm's place. Then she turned to make her way toward the hospital.

It was hot walking over the dry earth, skirting around the low hills in which the dugout warrens of men were hidden and turning smartly aside when a fast-traveling, spiraling willy-willy would have choked her in a swirl of red dust.

But she couldn't turn aside from the steady wind that scarcely ever ceased to blow, except for that short period in the morning and evening, and which was blowing now, driving the dust. It was as though the world was being pulverized into fine powder to fill the nostrils. At least, there would be no dust like this in Grandma Birch's street.

Then she remembered. They might never go to Grandma Birch's street now, never meet those nice young people next door. These were not pleasant thoughts and she was thankful when the hospital came into view.

As she opened the fly-wire door onto the veranda, she heard a small child's giggle. Then as soon as the dazzle of sunlight went from her eyes she saw Ruthie and Kathy both sitting on the polished floor in the cool passage. Kathy was rolling a bright red ball over the tiles to the baby girl, who was thrusting it back with her long arms and fingers.

Kathy looked up quickly at the visitor and though her eyes welcomed Liz with a quick shine, her lips did not part in a smile. She was still hiding the gap in her front teeth.

"Hello," Liz said, and dropped down onto the floor beside Ruthie, whose smile and giggle faded. But she didn't cry, only moved on those thin legs, quick as a scuttling beetle, to Kathy and climbed headfirst onto her lap, pressing her nose into the dark girl's middle. She clung there, turning her head a fraction so that she could peer at Liz out of a parting in the curtain of lashes.

"At least she didn't yell," Liz said, crossing her legs.

"She's gained a whole pound this week," Kathy told her eagerly. "Sister says it's because I've looked after her well. D'ye know, Liz, she says I'm good with kids."

Kathy also looked as though she might have gained a

pound or two in the week. She was wearing one of Sister's own cotton frocks, a floral cotton that was different from anything Liz had ever seen her in, far different from the shapeless tent that George Murphy had bought for ten cents and different from the blue uniform supplied by the Reserve. In this dress of Sister's—in a style that Liz herself often wore—she looked older and more assured.

With some surprise, Liz decided that Kathy was probably not much younger than herself. Somehow, because Kathy's schoolwork was years below her own, she had always thought of her as very much younger and, probably because of this, had mothered her. But that this was a wrong assumption was made evident by this dress, by the well-brushed hair and shining skin. She was pretty, Liz thought, with those soft dark eyes and features that were Aboriginal but not over-heavy.

"Reckoned you might come today," Kathy said, offhand, still trying not to grin. "Sister says Ruthie's smart. Knows to bawl now if I don't pick her up as soon as she wants."

"Don't spoil her," said Liz automatically. "She'll miss you when you leave the hospital."

Kathy's face clouded. "What you think about me when you leave Opal Town—that I miss you? What I do when you leave, Liz?"

Liz had been going to tell her that she mightn't be going to leave, that she might never leave the Opal Town now, but just then Sister Joan, looking crisp as usual, came from the kitchen, and the words died. She couldn't give Sister Joan any hint of what she had in mind, in case she passed it on to Mr. Robbins. He would be very angry and disappointed if she did anything to ruin her chances of acquiring the training that would make her a teacher.

Sister Joan had a small bowl of custard in her hand.

"Hello, Liz. Glad to see you. Kathy looks better, doesn't she? The swelling's nearly gone. I'll let her go back to school about the middle of next week. In the meantime, I'm finding her a great help with Ruthie. The young monkey eats better when Kathy feeds her than with me. Will you give her this custard now, Kathy?"

With self-conscious pride, Kathy swung herself and the child upright, Ruthie burrowing into her neck. She carried her to the kitchen, put her into a highchair and carefully adjusted the safety straps over her shoulders.

Then she took the bowl of custard from Sister Joan and started to feed the baby with a spoon. She was careful to scrape the underside of the spoon against the top edge of the bowl so that no adhering custard dropped on the clean floor and careful to guide the spoon gently into the baby's mouth. The whole operation was solemn and meticulous, and Ruthie was just as solemn. Apparently being fed by Kathy was regarded by her as right and proper.

"Don't she eat nice?" Kathy demanded of Liz. "Good as Mrs. Jim's kid?"

"Just as good."

"Sister Joan's going to teach me to make custard. Very good, she says, for big bellies and skinny legs. Can you make custard, Liz?"

Liz had to admit she couldn't, British history and mathematics having taken up too much of her time to date.

Then she heard the outside door shut and male voices on the veranda.

"Steve and Bill," she told Kathy, and that was when the first spoonful didn't reach the baby's mouth but somehow slipped sideways and landed on the floor.

The voices hovered on the veranda until Sister Joan called out, "You may come in. We're in the kitchen."

The two boys came down the passage with a tiptoe kind of gait. After all, this was a hospital, and a hospital meant chloroform and silence. They had been somewhat disappointed that no whiff of the drug met them at the door. They didn't often have an excuse to visit this strange clean sanctum and felt they were cheated by not being met at the door by that unseen but exciting odor of insensibility. And Kathy, the patient, not even in bed, but feeding Ruthie!

"Hello, Kathy," said Bill.

"Hello," said Steve.

Kathy said "Hello" through closed lips.

"Show us your tooth," said Bill, not knowing what else to say.

"Haven't got it."

"No—I mean, show us the hole."

Kathy turned her head away.

"Bill!" Liz cried. "What a thing to ask!"

"Well-l . . ." Bill glowered at his sister. Schoolmarm again! Making him feel he was about as old as Ruthie.

Steve balanced from one foot to the next. He waved a hand at the baby, grinning. "Reckon she's grown."

Kathy brightened at once but she didn't smile. "Yes. She likes the way I feed her."

"Seem to be doing pretty good."

"D'ye think so?" Kathy was so pleased that she almost opened her mouth wide, but remembered in time and muttered the words through stiff lips.

"Reckon we better go," said Bill.

"Yer just got here," protested Kathy, having established

her ability, "and you can see Ruthie drink a glass of milk now. Never spill a drop."

"Huh-h . . ." said Bill. "Why should she spill it?"

"It's clever," said Steve, "when you're as little as that."

Kathy picked up the glass and looked from one to the other of her audience, eyes dancing with achievement yet so self-conscious that Liz was sure if there had been a desk handy she'd have slid under it. But there was no desk, and so she held the glass to the baby's lips, held it firmly until two spidery hands grasped it tightly and Ruthie began to drink.

"See . . . ?" Kathy said proudly, and she had to smile then, revealing the gap, large and ugly, like the entrance to an inner cavern in her mouth.

"Gee!" said Bill. "Must have been a whopping tooth!"

But Steve said, "She's a good drinker, Kathy—just like you said."

"Better go now," urged Bill. "We're only making dusty marks on the floor. You wriggle your feet an awful lot, Steve."

Steve looked down at his stockman's elastic-sided boots. "Yeah," he agreed.

"C'mon." Bill was edging out of the kitchen into the passage, eager to be gone. No chloroform. No patient moaning in delirium. Only Ruthie eating custard and drinking milk, which was a very poor show.

"C'mon . . ." Bill was halfway up the passage, his mind already leaping ahead to tomorrow and wondering whether he had "borrowed" enough gelignite for the job.

Steve stood awkwardly for a moment, looking from Kathy to the baby girl. "You're doing a good job," he repeated. "Looks different, doesn't she, now she's clean?"

"She's not going back to Margaret," Kathy said suddenly. "Margaret don't keep her like this. Sister says she just get big belly and skinny legs again if she goes back."

Steve stood, easing his weight from one foot to the other.

From the passage Bill called, "C'mon."

Liz stepped back a little. Somehow, what Kathy was saying was meant for Steve alone. Kathy was talking about her people—his people—their people.

Kathy sighed. "I wish Margaret knew how to make custard. Then Ruthie would be all right."

And Sister Joan, who had been quietly busy at the sink, said, "Once you've learned, Kathy, you can teach Margaret. She will learn, maybe, from you."

"Yeah—that's it," said Steve. "You learn an' teach Margaret. Maybe the kid could stay with her then."

"D'ye think I could teach her?" cried Kathy, then she frowned. "But she hasn't got a nice stove pot like Sister's —and even if she had one, it'd get awfully black over the campfire."

"Learn anyway," advised Steve, "and maybe you could look after Ruthie. I gotta go—Bill's waiting."

"Yes, get my brother out of here," cried Liz with relief. "He's the wrong kind to come visiting in hospitals—even when there aren't any sick patients."

It was after the boys had gone and Kathy had been given the task of putting Ruthie down to sleep that Sister Joan talked quietly to Liz.

"Those two—Steve and Kathy—are going to be like soldiers in the front line of battle, a kind of spearhead," she said, almost thinking aloud.

Liz's eyes questioned the Sister.

"For their people, I mean. It's hard to do much for the older ones, Liz. I've tried. But they're suspicious of what white people offer and you can't blame them. They've had little reason to trust us in the past, and many of us are not to be trusted in the present. But young ones like Steve and Kathy who can see some reason and reward in living as you and I do, Liz, and who *want* to have better lives are going to lead the rest of their people to better lives."

Liz still looked a little uncomprehending, and Sister Joan went on.

"By example, I mean. And not just *our* Steve and Kathy —there'll be others, too. Not that it will be easy for them. They'll often be discouraged and hurt by us—and some will stop trying and fail. But those who succeed—who find a respected place in our community—will do more for their people than we can ever do, Liz."

Liz knew that Sister Joan was speaking from experience, that she had indeed tried hard to teach the dark women who noodled a living on the opal fields a better way to cook, a better way to care for their children, a better way to live.

"They have to *want* what we offer," she repeated and then smiled at Liz. "You've given Kathy the incentive to want to be like you—to do things the way you do them. That's why she's willing to learn—why I'll be able to teach her. Kathy was lucky to meet you, Liz—and Steve was lucky to be taken into Carl's care." Then she added sadly, "Unfortunately, it doesn't happen to many of the Aborigines."

From the nursery ward came the sound of Kathy and Ruthie giggling together.

Sister Joan said, "I'm going to enjoy teaching Kathy—I know it will be worthwhile."

Liz had always known that Sister Joan felt deeply about the Aboriginal people, but now she understood why she was prepared to stay on in this harsh climate and heat. And she understood, too, why Mr. Robbins was so angry when any of his Aboriginal pupils missed school. A kind of spearhead . . .

"Your part has been more important than you realize, Liz," Sister Joan said.

Liz blushed. She had never thought of it that way. It was just that she had liked Kathy and Kathy had liked her. But now, as she turned to leave, she knew that it wasn't going to be nearly as hard to put her own ambitions back a year.

14

An Old Windlass

IT WASN'T easy for Liz to escape the dugout that Sunday morning. Her mother looked at her with questioning eyes.

"Why should you want to visit Old Welhelm today, when there's all that study to do?" she demanded, in a voice that was sharp and high-pitched because she was tired.

May hadn't slept much last night, nor Mike either. He had been very quiet after returning from Carl's, telling her in few words how his parcel had been found by others. But May had felt the explosive content of his mind, the bitter anger that he had been unfairly beaten in a race, the crippling sense that time, too, was defeating him, that he wouldn't be given another chance.

He hadn't expressed any of this in words, but his silence had been harder to bear than the blast from his tongue which would have relieved his tension. May had even tried to ignite that pent-up gas, but without success. Never before had she felt so distant from Mike, as though they were indeed no longer on the same road.

152

It was a frightening thought and one which she only vaguely understood. After all, he must know—in fact, he had always said—that their time in the Opal Town must, of necessity, be limited. And what could limit it more effectively, or bring it to an end more definitely, than the need of their child, their daughter, to find *her* place in the world—a world of learning and, in turn, a world in which to give out that learning? To live, too; to get to know other boys and girls of her own age, to enjoy being sixteen and young. Surely Mike knew this, had always known it. Liz had to have her life, and there was no life for her here in the Opal Town.

But May did wish that she had never mentioned hairdos or roses. He hadn't said so, but perhaps he was holding these personal ambitions of hers against her, for the first time shutting his mind and silencing his tongue against sharing this bitter disappointment.

And now, if Liz was suddenly going to treat her study lightly, as though passing that all-important exam no longer mattered, how was she going to continue to justify to Mike the need to leave this place?

May felt bewildered and hurt by her daughter's offhand "I'm not studying today, Mum." The slam of the door, as Liz and Bill and Potch went out into the unusually hot still air, struck a blow on her already throbbing head. Mike and Liz—unlike Bill—were always so close to her, part of her, but they were behaving this morning as though she was not *part of them.* Behaving as though they were living lives in which she didn't figure—Mike buttoning his disappointment into that tight bitter mind, and Liz going off, with equally tight mouth, as though there was nothing strange or entirely new in this repudiation of British history and mathematics.

May had intended, once again, to cook a round of roast beef for this Sunday's midday dinner, as Grandma Birch would do, but what was the use if Liz and Bill weren't there to eat it, and Mike so uninterested in food that a cup of tea sufficed for his breakfast?

And Welhelm—of all people—why Old Welhelm?

But Liz, actually, didn't go into Welhelm's dugout. This was to save time. She was a favorite with Welhelm, mainly because her yellow hair and blue eyes reminded him of his own Nordic roots and made him a little nostalgic for the girl he had left behind in Sweden fifty-odd years earlier.

Welhelm's dugout was a small man-made cave and his bed-cubicle was not excavated to the same height as the rest of it, so that he slept with either his feet or his head, depending on the weather, under a shelf of rock only a couple of feet above. If it was hot he put his feet under the ledge, in cold weather his head.

But hot or cold, he always wore a thick flannel shirt and long serge trousers. And he thanked God that he could still gouge enough opal in the various shafts that surrounded his dugout to prevent his getting the old-age pension.

"I'll be old," he said, at seventy-eight, "when I have to get the old-age pension."

Liz loved Old Welhelm, who had received a degree from a Swedish university but had had the opal fever with unabated heat for nearly fifty years, and she loved to listen to his stories. But not today. Learning of any kind was to be shunned today. In any case, Bill was in command of the day's work and had said, "We're not stopping while you gas to Old Welhelm."

So he had gone alone to borrow the old man's bicycle, which was seldom used now, for Welhelm's wind and leg muscles were not what they were. Other old-timers, who drove vehicles, brought out his supplies.

It was a rusty machine, with leaking tire valves, and every half-mile Steve had to get off and pump up the tires. It was a bumpy, noisy ride. The picks and shovels clattered together on their backs and the twelve-gallon bucket—borrowed from Old Welhelm—which Liz had to carry was heavy. They clattered along over the stones, and because each stone threw off its own reflected heat it was like riding in an oven.

As Bill was dinking his sister, Steve balanced Potch for most of the way on a folded Hessian bag in front of him. Potch rode with a pained expression and his body stiff. When an occasional vehicle passed them with a dog sitting proudly on the bench seat beside his master, Potch pretended he didn't see or hear the other animal's derisive barking.

A dog of the Opal Town that belonged to a man was very different from one of the pack. Such a dog was a man's mate—he ate and drank as well as his master, and was free to voice a passing opinion.

It seemed a long, long journey out to the Greek Patch, and Potch was as pleased as his mates to reach the end.

Being Sunday, not many men were working on the field. Most had gone to their dugouts or their tents or their shacks to do their washing, or to the store to buy food and gelignite. There was just an odd winch or windlass turning here and there, but to their great dissatisfaction old Melikos was busy around his mine-head, together with one of his men, a young fellow called Rigas, and Nikos.

Their usual uninterested façade was disturbed by the trundling bikes, one whining with a rusty beat. Even old Melikos smiled at Liz's dangling legs and the noisy bucket, at the way she had to scramble off when Bill could trundle over the workings no longer and the way they had to pick their steps, weighed down with bikes and gear, to the top of the shaft of Eldorado.

However, the new arrivals had one thing at least to be thankful for—none of the encircling shafts was working. Looking across at the silent rubble around the north claim, it was hard to realize that opal history had been made there yesterday.

But it was rather embarrassing when Potch spotted Nikos and set off at a run to greet the boy. Bill had to call him back smartly.

Bill announced then that the first thing to do was to pick up the old hand-driven windlass from a mine a quarter of a mile away.

"We'll need your help to carry it, Liz," he said. "It's bound to be heavy, and the quicker we get it here the quicker we'll be able to put in that monkey."

Liz didn't argue. She had promised to go along with this idea, and go along she must; but she knew that the Melikos group was laughing loudly when the three of them came back struggling with the unwieldy contraption.

They carried it with its legs stuck up in the air, so that it looked like a dead horse, except that it seemed to have so many more legs, sticking out at sharp angles from the horizontal winding-barrel, than the usual four. When they turned it right side up, these legs poked at her shins and her knees, barked her ankles, filled her fingers with splinters and screwed her back into a peculiar angle.

It was a very old windlass, constructed in the days when there had been a few pockets of mulga in the area. But the mulga had long disappeared, used for shoring up a shaft, building a humpy or just firewood.

Liz looked at the barrel and saw that age and heat had opened fine cracks in the wood. It was a thin barrel, too, evidently designed for use by a one-man team. She had to voice her doubt. "Are you sure it'll be safe, Bill? It has to take you down seventy feet."

His eyes snapped "Schoolmarm again!" and his tongue said, "Of course it's safe. Mulga's the toughest wood in the world—never wears out. What about the cottage on Boobook Station—those logs are more than a hundred years old."

"Yes," said Liz faintly, "but what about the rope?"

"You don't think we'd use that old rope, do you? Steve's got a brand new rope lashed to his bike."

Liz kept quiet after that and tried to do what she could to help while the boys pushed and patted and thrust the windlass into position. Fortunately, it straddled their hole with a good firm stride and certainly looked sturdy enough once established. Then Steve fixed the rope he had carried on his bike in position while Bill and Liz prepared the fuse for the charges, snipping off each length with a clean cut.

Liz was not ignorant of mining operations. Until she was nearly as old as Bill, she had taken some interest in mining proceedings, if only for the sake of escape from the confines of the dugout and the Opal Town. She knew how to prepare a charge and how to let it off. Nevertheless, she hoped that she wouldn't be asked to go down into the shaft.

Bill had decided to put down two monkeys within a few feet of each other in the same drive.

"We'll need a dozen charges," he said. "Six in each. That's not like the forty or fifty Dad sometimes lets off, and the fumes should clear pretty quickly—by the time we've eaten our lunch, anyway."

"The air's very still—no wind," Liz observed, but diffidently. "Do you think the fumes will clear in the time?"

Bill refused to answer this further dampening question. But Steve said, "Pity your dad took the air sock away."

"Pity he took away any of the gear—especially the ladders!" Bill said, still disgusted. "I just can't understand why he gave up so easily."

"Hard hit," Steve sympathized. "He and Carl were going out to the Gidgee Field this afternoon to look for another spot."

"Dad's not going to feel very happy about any other spot—he believed this one was special. Now—you and I'll go down and bore the holes for the charges, Steve. We have two augers so that shouldn't take long. Then you can man the windlass ready to bring me and Liz up after we light the fuse."

Liz looked sharply at her brother. "I didn't think you'd need me down the hole."

"Of course I'll need you down the hole. It has to be either you or Steve, for the sake of speed. And it's better for Steve to be on the windlass then, because he'll bring us up so much quicker."

"How high is the drive?" Liz tried not to sound perturbed. She reminded herself that Steve was going down, and she knew how *he* felt about those dark depths that were silent and cool and away from all living things. In any case, Bill was in the kind of mood that would stand no argument.

"You won't have to crawl in." Bill was impatient. "You'll be able to stand almost upright. I don't know why you don't like holes—after all, you live in one!"

This was true, but the dugout was roomy, airy, easy of access and exit. It never seemed like a hole.

He added, "If it's the gelly you're frightened of, I'll light them all myself, and you can stay up here with Steve."

"No!" Such cowardice would be hard to live down, even though she knew, and he knew, that her young brother was pushing her to the limit. He could indeed light them all himself.

She understood that this was, perhaps subconsciously, his form of revenge for the anguish of mind for which he held her responsible. In any case, the thing she feared was not the explosive or the hole itself, but the weight of the earth.

Liz lowered first one boy and then the other. Each stood on the sling to go down, holding onto the rope with one hand and carrying an auger and a carbide lamp in the other. The augers looked as though they could do with sharpening. It would take muscle to push those rasping bits through the sandstone, very different from the way the jackhammer, driven by the compressor, bit through the rock. The evil-smelling carbide lamps, too, would not light the vault as electricity had done, and when they came to raise the stone, lack of a power hoist would restrict them to the use of the twelve-gallon bucket.

The windlass creaked at the joints as the sling spiraled down, but as the barrel was not a heavy one Liz was able to turn it with reasonable ease. Once her charges were below, she sat on the pile of rubble to await their signal to be brought up. Flies, tiny buzzing machines that whirred into eyes, nose, ears and mouth, tormented her and for once she wished for the wind that at least would have kept them on the lee side of her.

Across the mound of the shaft on the east side of Eldorado, Melikos and his two helpers were busy strengthening the mouth of their shaft. Every now and again the younger man, Rigas, would look across and laugh, and she fancied once, wretchedly, that she heard that hateful word, hunch. She was relieved when she saw Rigas set off over the workings to where a countryman labored in the distance.

A few minutes later the boys signaled to be brought up. Both were sweating after boring those holes through two feet of sandstone with blunt augers. The next task was to put in the charges.

Steve looked somewhat doubtful as Bill slipped the sticks of gelignite into the bucket and the detonators into his pocket while Liz picked up the lengths of yellow fuse.

"Don't reckon Liz should go down when she doesn't like holes—especially to light fuse . . ." It was unlike Steve to be critical of any proposal of Bill's.

"It'll be cooler down there—and no flies," Liz snapped before Bill could answer. She was determined now that if her going down the shaft was going to make him feel better, then she was going down. "In any case, we've got six feet of fuse for each shot, which is much more than Dad uses. That gives us three minutes to light them all and get to the top. If you can't get us out in three minutes, Steve, there'll be something wrong."

"Don't like it . . ." muttered Steve. "Better if I'm down there."

"No," said Bill. "You know as well as I do that we must have a good man on the windlass when we're letting off gelly—especially with no ladders."

So Steve stopped arguing and lowered first Bill and then Liz.

Liz sat in the sling and thought what a long, long way down it was—seventy feet—spiraling ever faster and faster, the walls seeming to move in as though closing over her head as she went lower. Bill was waiting at the bottom with both carbide lamps lit, and she forced her eyes to stay on this bright gleam. Down, down, down. Then her dangling feet touched bottom. Bill helped her disentangle from the chair and gave her a lamp to carry. One quick look upward revealed the sky still there, but only as a tiny blue oblong shape immensely high above them.

Bill left the bucket at the bottom of the shaft and carried the bundle of gelignite in his hand. Liz followed behind, keeping her eye on his back and stifling the thought that now the gray-white walls were leaning in on her.

The boys had chosen a spot about thirty feet in along the drive to put down their first "monkey," and soon they came to the twelve holes bored in the floor of the drive with the augers. Each was surrounded by a little pile of pulverized stone and looked like the holes of giant borer beetles.

Quickly Bill set to work to fit the detonators to the fuse, nipping each cap tightly to one end with a pair of crimping pliers and pressing the shining metal cylinder—about a quarter-inch in diameter and two inches long—into the top of the stick of gelignite until it looked like a pink candle with a long yellow wick. Then he began to ease the candle down into the hole bored into the rock, pushing it down the two-feet depth of the spider-hole with a piece of broomstick left behind by his father. He knew better than to use an iron bar to ram the charge into position.

They were putting down two monkeys and the holes had been bored with some precision—three on either side about a foot apart and the other set about six feet distant. Presently all that could be seen in the light of the carbides were the twelve lengths of fuse snaking over the thick white dust on the floor of the drive.

Liz breathed deeply when the last was rammed home. After those first moments of following Bill, she had found that she could stand upright and some of her fears of the pressing-in walls evaporated. She was thinking now only of the job they had to do.

"I'll light the farthest six," Bill said briskly, taking two fuse-lighters from his pocket and applying a match to each. "You do the six nearest the shaft, and then run for it."

Liz took the six-inch fuse-lighter—like a thin brown cigar—from her brother's hand and set to work, not even jumping when the first fuse hissed alight. Once the first fuse was asmolder there was no time to waste. They had just the amount of time that the first fuse took to burn down to the detonator in which to ignite all the rest, get clear and be hauled to the top. Burning time of the fuse was recognized as two feet a minute.

Liz worked now as coolly as her young brother. Strangely enough, she had suddenly lost all sense of being hemmed in, of encroaching walls, of being buried in the depth of the earth. The knowledge elated her. She would tell Bill when they reached the surface.

She went from one fuse to the next. She had been brought up with the boom of explosives in her ears and, though she had been taught a healthy respect for gelignite, familiarity forbade fear now. Certainly she had never been below in a drive before or actually set off a charge, but she had seen it done often enough in the shallow workings before she had become too studious and grown-up.

Although she was cool and handling her fuse-lighter as easily as Bill, the lighting of these charges seemed like a ritual. They were going to blast away this rock to reveal—what? Nothing, probably, as their father said. And the year ahead for all of them would still be so different from what had been planned.

"Hurry!" Bill urged. "You look as though you're lighting birthday candles."

"I have to be sure they're lit!" she retorted as she sprang to the next. Then she stood poised for a moment, noting the curl of smoke coming from each fuse. "I've finished!"

"Hop to it then!" Bill was a man down here in the dungeon of the earth, a man who knew the ways of gelignite with sandstone. "Go on! Get!"

Liz turned toward the entrance to the drive. She was able to run because she could almost stand upright in this man-made tunnel. Bill was right behind her, almost knocking into her. She could see the sling dangling ahead in the shaft, lit by the daylight coming in at the top. How long before the first boom?

"Keep going!" Bill cried.

She grasped the sling and Bill helped her to sit on the narrow iron bar. She was not like the boys who were used to spiraling upward with one foot in the sling or the bucket, clasping the rope. Then she signaled and Steve began to turn the windlass. Already strong smoke from the burning fuse was whirling toward them.

Up, up, up.

But she had not gone many feet before there was a sudden sharp snap from above—a shout from Steve—and Liz fell like a stone, back to the floor of the shaft.

Because she was sitting in the sling, she fell heavily, grazing the side of the bucket in which they had carried down the gelignite, and the rope snaked down after her, draping around her shoulders.

"Liz!" Bill cried. The next instant he was picking up the bucket, thrusting it at her. "Put it on!" he screamed.

Winded, Liz could only look at him.

"Put it on! Over your head!"

Stupidly, she looked at him.

Then he upended it himself and thrust it down over her yellow hair. Dust from the bottom of it filled her eyes, her nostrils, shut out the light and almost suffocated her. All the agony of being in an enclosed space returned and swept over her. She wanted to kick at the bucket with her feet, to kick her way out of the darkness, to fight it off with her hands. But she only banged her head against the iron sides and hurt her ears as she fought.

Then Bill pushed her forward, hard into the wall of the shaft. She felt him fling himself down beside her, felt him burrow his head down at her side.

Suddenly there was a deep heavy boom. She felt the world shake, the stone wall quiver, heard the thump as a piece of flying rock struck the bucket.

"Bill!" she cried, her voice lost in the bucket. "That's only the first!"

She couldn't hear whether he answered, but he moved beside her.

She said again, "That's *one!*"

There were another eleven to follow. She had to count them. Miners always counted the shots. They had to know, for safety's sake, if they all went off.

That was only the first explosion, and rock had hit the

bucket! And Bill had no such covering. She wanted to tear this dreadful black casing away to see what was happening to Bill.

Then came the second boom. More rock, more dust, and now the fumes. The choking gelignite fumes that—breathed sufficiently into the lungs—could be lethal, even twenty-four hours later.

Ten to go.

Three gone . . . Only seconds between now. And rocks flying and the earth shaking as though the seventy feet of rock above them must surely break into pieces and fall —and fumes that choked—and Bill moving beside her. She held onto him tightly and stretched as far as she could over him, hoping that the bucket might shield him, too.

That was four . . . five . . .

Seven to go.

The rumble was all around them, ricocheting from one wall of the shaft to the other, smashing onto the tin, off again, and back. Each time it hit the bucket it seemed to pierce her eardrums. They pained and echoed with the on-slaught, so that it was hard to count the true shots now. The reverberating noise and movement were as encom-passing as a blanket, filling her ears with sound and her nostrils with the choking smell. Eight . . . nine . . . ten . . .

The loud noise and sharp movement were all around, at-tacking her, yet becoming vague like a shadow booming; her head was beginning to throb from the poisonous fumes.

Were there two to go or three?

Was that last one eleven or twelve?

She heard Bill speak from a long way off, in a strange brittle voice, "That's it! That's the lot! With no wind— Steve had better get us up quick!"

15

Seventy Feet Down

But at the top of the shaft Steve was lying sprawled beside the hole, his eyes closed. The snap of the wooden barrel in the windlass had flung a broken end at him and struck him on the head. He didn't even know that the rope which was to have brought his friends up to safety had coiled at the bottom of the shaft.

But Potch knew that something was wrong, that Steve shouldn't be lying so still and useless. He looked at Steve, licked him several times, barked down into the dark hole of the shaft and twitched his nose at the peculiar smell that was rising. His tail began to droop. Something was wrong. This strange inactivity, after the bustling of the last few hours—and Bill down there, and the smell. He knew Bill was down there because he had seen him go and had wanted to go with him.

His bark changed to a series of staccato yelps and presently Nikos, who had turned his back on those who had once been his friends, felt impelled to turn again and look.

167

At first he thought they must have all gone below, and Potch was barking because he had been left behind. He couldn't see Steve lying below the rim of the rubble.

Then suddenly Potch seemed to remember that he was not alone on the field with his frightening problem, that Nikos whom he knew so well was just across the stony workings. He began to run toward Nikos—half-way, three-parts of the way, then back to the shaft. Back and forth. Barking ever louder and louder and with ever-increasing urgency as the smell from the shaft became stronger.

That was when Nikos, risking his father's temper, left his post. Nikos's father was not digging for opal on this Sunday but had gone below to retrieve a pick that needed a handle and also to inspect the hole he had been gouging when work finished yesterday, and Nikos was waiting for the signal to say that he was ready to come up. Now he turned and sprinted across the rubble and rough ground to Eldorado. He went close enough to see the broken windlass and Steve sprawled on the ground. The sight of Steve jerked him to a sudden stop. How badly hurt was he? But even as he stared, Steve moved a leg, so Nikos turned and raced back to his own mine.

Although he was not a runner, it took him only seconds to cover the distance. Sensing what had happened, he realized that Bill and Liz must be down in the shaft, breathing the fumes of the twelve charges. He knew there were twelve because, from habit, he had counted the number of dull booming reverberations.

He sent his own signal down to his father—a frantic tugging of the rope that clanged the bell at the bottom of the shaft. And he called.

"Pappa! Pappa!"

Pappa Melikos recognized the urgency and, though he was far in from the shaft opening, sprang immediately for the streak of light from the mine head.

When he signaled that he heard, Nikos pulled him to the top of the shaft. The boy waved an arm at Eldorado to indicate the barking dog and broke into rapid Greek.

"*Thistihima!—afti ine eke kato!*"

His father threw up his hands with a sharp word.

Nikos said, "Barrel broke—they're caught down there!"

"Who? How many?"

"The boy and the girl. Bill and Liz."

Melikos let off a round grunt that could have been anger or could have been concern. But he moved smartly —this time toward his utility. Jumping into the driving seat, he moved the vehicle, with a quick swish through the gears, as near to the shaft of Eldorado as the workings would allow. Then he took a great length of tough rope from the tray, tied it around the front axle and climbed fast over the rubble toward the broken windlass. Here he stopped only long enough to take one look at Steve, who was trying to open an eye, and to send one huge shout across to Rigas and his other countryman, Manolis, a couple of hundred yards away.

"They come!" he told Nikos succinctly. "By the time they get here, I have the first ready to pull up. You help them."

From the pocket of his shorts he drew a piece of rag that he used to wipe the sweat from his neck and tied it over his nose. Then he swung over the side, skidding down the rope that strained from the utility. He was a short but powerful man and his years with the Greek Resistance Forces had toughened and molded his body to a highly disciplined machine. Nikos was proud of the way his father went down that rope.

Potch was quieter now, still barking at intervals but aware that something was being done for Bill who was down there with that strange alarming smell. In between, he licked Steve's face, urging him to wake up. And Steve was waking up, pushing himself up on one elbow, his eyes dull and his face puckered in wonderment at finding himself stretched out on the stones. Then he sat up and slowly rubbed the side of his head where it hurt.

Potch sprang at him then, nearly knocking him flat again but at least bringing him to full consciousness.

Steve saw Nikos standing there, the rope already in his hand for the first pull. When Nikos looked back at him with one dark eye made darker by the ring of faded bruise around it, Steve saw that Bill's blow had indeed connected. Bill would be very pleased about that—he hadn't liked being beaten by Nikos.

That made Steve wonder why he was lying down, what had happened and indeed what *was* happening, and he rubbed harder at his bruised head.

"Pappa—he's gone down," Nikos said. "He'll get them."

Then Rigas and the other miner sprang onto the rubble and in a few words Nikos explained what had happened. The men took a grip on the rope and waited for the signal from below. Rigas was smiling; he and Melikos and Manolis and Nikos, of course, would bring the unfortunate ones to safety.

They didn't talk now, just waited. Except for an occasional whimper Potch, too, was silent.

Then the tug came. Hand over hand, Nikos and the two

miners began to pull up the rope. Not too quickly, not too roughly, for they couldn't be sure of the condition of Liz and Bill. If they were unconscious, rough handling would bump them mercilessly against the stone walls.

It was Liz's head and face that appeared first—streaked with dirt and white beneath the streaks. But her eyes were open—bleary and shocked, but open. She was sitting in the loop that Melikos had made in the end of the rope, tied firmly to the rope as well and using her right hand to keep her dangling legs from contact with the sandstone walls.

In a moment, Rigas had untied Melikos's knots and pulled Liz free. He helped her carefully to a seat on the stones beside Steve while Nikos sent the rope slithering below again.

There was another wait, during which Liz could only clasp her knees and resist the temptation to rise and peer down the shaft after Bill. She knew her legs were without strength and her head was throbbing enough to send her crashing again to the bottom if she leaned over the shaft.

So she clasped her knees as tight as she could and waited.

After a time—the longest period of time she had ever known—Bill's head appeared and then his shoulders. His eyes, too, were open and he was conscious enough to have protected his slowly revolving body with its bare legs from the grating walls. But he was not, perhaps, in quite such good shape as Liz. There were a number of cuts on his forehead and head, and his hands were scratched where he had used them to protect his face against the flying stone.

He, too, was put down with the same care beside his sister and Steve, while Nikos, Rigas and Manolis raised the heavier bulk of Melikos to the surface. While they waited, Potch shivered with joy and pressed his comforting body into Bill's back.

Melikos was coughing when he reached the top but stepped smartly from the sling, planting himself firmly in front of three scarred and shaken opal miners.

"Foolish!" he said, in his deep Greek tone. "Foolish! You have no sense." He waved toward the old decrepit windlass. "You not try for strength or cracks before you use? That is old—old as me, perhaps. And you use it! Seventy feet down you go—on that thing! And after gelly— with no wind!"

Bill studied a stubbed big toe and scratched legs, and was glad to feel Potch pressing into his back. It had been a horrifying few minutes down there, with the booming gelly seeming to explode in and tear his eardrums, feeling the quake of the earth, the terrifying whizz of fragments of blasted stone, the choking dust—and then smelling the fumes. Those deadly poisonous fumes. He had feared the fumes more than the flying stones, feared for what might happen to Liz who was down there because of him.

He knew he hadn't examined that windlass—he who prided himself on being a good miner—not even when Liz questioned its strength; nor had he heeded her query about lack of wind.

That was why he was glad to feel Potch pressing close. Potch was the only one who wouldn't blame him.

"Where your pappa that he let you go down? Let you disobey law? You have no license to use the gelly."

"He didn't know we were going down."

Melikos shrugged, spreading his hands. "So! This what happens. You Australians—no discipline. Pappa not boss. Now you half dead. S'pose I have to take you home."

Bill shivered. Old Melikos—take them home!

"We've got bikes," he said.

"And your sister? She able to ride bike?"

Bill looked at Liz. No, she certainly didn't look as though she could ride a bike, or even be dinked.

"And Steve? He no better than the pair of you. Had a good whack on the head."

"We'll be grateful for a ride," Liz said.

Old Melikos smiled then. "Your brother care for you well," he conceded. "He not so bad for no discipline—think quickly. What the words—'quick on the up-take'—that's good. That bucket save you bad scratches like he got, and save your ears from being blasted off. Now," he eyed Liz, "I carry you."

He picked her up as though she were weightless, while Rigas helped the groggy Steve to his feet, supporting him with his shoulder, and Nikos quietly turned to help Bill.

It was then that Bill noted the lingering traces of the black eye, and Nikos looked quickly away.

"Don't tell him—my pappa—you hit me," Nikos said. "I didn't tell him it was you."

16

Mike Confronts Melikos

Liz and the two boys rode in the cabin of the utility with old Melikos. Potch crouched in the tray with the considerable gear that Melikos always seemed to carry, which meant that the bikes had to be left behind. It was a tight fit in the cabin, and the air was hot and heavy with the smell of sweaty bodies.

Liz's head felt enlarged, with heavy hammers beating in each separate cell in her brain, and she could see by the glassy look in Bill's eyes that he felt the same. The fumes had drugged the power to think out of him and perhaps it was just as well, for the next half hour could prove worse than the minutes spent in the exploding earth. Melikos taking them home! Melikos telling of the stupidity of their mining activities! Melikos being superior because he was the big pappa in his household and his sons and daughters did only what he allowed. How Mike would squirm when he had to thank Melikos for the prompt action that had saved his children and Steve, how angry he would be with them!

174

What with the throbbing and the smells and her thoughts, Liz began to feel violently sick.

Steve was the calmest. He had accepted the bandaging of the open cut on his head with Melikos's sweat rag, though protesting he needed nothing. "I've got an Aboriginal skull—like cast iron." He grinned, and was proud, Liz thought.

Bill just sat stiffly beside old Melikos. Though why the Greek should be called old, Liz was beginning to wonder.

He was probably at least ten years younger than her father, with a great capacity for work and a greater capacity to drive—or refuse—a hard bargain with any opal buyer. The whole field knew that Melikos was the spokesman, the seller, for his "company." And even an erratic grasp of English didn't prevent him from being a good seller. No, old Melikos was not old. He had many years yet to work in the field. It would make it harder for her father to thank him.

Liz hoped that Mike wouldn't be home when they arrived, that he and Carl would still be surveying their chances at the Gidgee Field where, it was rumored, there had been some good finds made lately. Good in quantity, that is, rather than quality. It was known that no truly precious durable opal came from the Gidgee—that some of the parcels found there were of the "cracky" type—but if the deposits were large enough it could still be a valuable find.

Despite the heat and the jabbing in her back from the broken spring in the upholstery, the nine-mile journey ended far too quickly for Liz. As they began to climb the steep ramp to the Watsons' dugout, she saw, with increased sickness, that her father's utility was standing outside the fly-wire door. It would have been better if they had had May alone to face. May would only be grateful for their safe return—she would not care who had saved them.

Melikos's utility found the steep track heavy going and the loud roar of the engine brought Mike to the fly-wire door. He peered through the wire for a second. Then, as though he were Bill, he pushed it open and allowed it to bang shut behind him as he stepped forth.

"What the dickens . . ." he began.

Steve was first to jump from the vehicle, bandage bloody and askew, then Potch jumped from the tray, barking joyously, happy to be home and unaware that Mike and Melikos were bitter enemies. Then Bill, more slowly, and Liz—still white-faced, dirty and with head too heavy to carry—clambered to the ground.

Melikos was slow in moving from the driver's seat, yet there was no diffidence in his manner as he faced Mike. There was even a half-smile beneath the clipped mustache. He stood with hands on his powerful hips, his bare torso shining in the sun.

"I brought 'em," he said. "Reckon they'll be all right."

"What d'ye mean?" Mike was snarling. All the hate he held for this man was welling up into his eyes, into his throat, into the tight-drawn lips. He took a step forward, fists at his sides but clenched.

Liz forced herself to move quickly despite her throbbing head. "Dad—he saved us!"

Mike turned sharply, and he answered. "What are you saying?" But his ears were not with the girl.

"Dad, he went down into Eldorado for us. We might have died of the fumes, but he was so quick. Please, Dad—listen to me, please understand."

"I don't understand anything," he said deliberately, and his blue eyes were black now, his lips a straight ugly line. He faced old Melikos—that arrogant Greek who held a Black Belt for karate in one hand and *his*, Mike's, parcel of opal in the other.

"I don't understand . . ." He wasn't trying to understand. He was trying to read Melikos's face, trying to see behind that bland, smooth, good-looking surface, almost sparring, for a moment or two, to gain time to coil the spring of his hate into a deadly weapon. This Melikos— boss of the company who had pegged him in—who had cut him off from that fortune of $100,000!

Only this morning, he and Carl had heard the amount from the opal buyer—a reputable man—who had bought the parcel. $100,000! He and Carl hadn't bothered to go out to the Gidgee then. Instead they'd gone to the store and bought a carton of beer—and they'd tried to drink away, in cold beer, the acrid taste of $100,000 missed. Missed by a couple of feet. No, by inches! And certainly only a couple of hours from their picks. And what was this Liz was saying? They might have died except for this Melikos? Died! She was sick, of course—eaten something perhaps. May would know—would be able to treat her.

"It's true, Dad!" Bill cried. "We went down into the mine. We put in a dozen shots, the windlass broke, and there were no ladders . . ."

"You went down the mine—and the windlass broke— and there were no ladders . . ." Mike repeated, but the words meant nothing to him. He was watching Melikos as he advanced slowly, savoring the moment when he would get his hands on the Greek. He wanted to savor it, to savor it to the full. $100,000! And it was in Melikos's hands. Slowly, a step at a time, he advanced.

"Dad!" Liz tried to quell the booming in her head. Then she ran to the wire door and banged on it. "Mum . . . Mum . . . quick! Mum-m-m!"

May came running, drying her hands on a tea towel.

Liz shouted, "He rescued us! Old Melikos rescued us. Dad doesn't understand. Stop him!"

May flung through the door and planted herself squarely between the two men. "You'd better listen, Mike!" she warned. "Listen to what Liz tells you! Listen . . ."

"I've listened long enough. One hundred thousand dollars' worth of listening!"

Melikos shrugged and stepped toward his utility. Turning down the corners of his mouth, he said, "It's of no matter."

"Wait, Mr. Melikos." May was almost regal with the sweep of her arm. "You can't go before I thank you. And I know I have to thank you—Liz said you rescued them. Let them tell me about it before you go."

"It was nothing." Melikos, plainly, was anxious now to go, even though Mike was no longer advancing but standing still in his tracks, bewildered.

"I'll tell you, Mum," Bill said quickly. "Steve and I reckoned we should put a monkey down in the drive. We pinched some gelignite from Dad's truck and we went out there today and let off the shots. But the windlass was old, and there were no ladders. The windlass broke—Liz and I were caught down there. Old . . . Mr. Melikos got cracking pretty smart and brought us up. And then— home . . ."

"Do you hear that, Mike?" May had lost the clip from her hair and she had to push the straight ends out of her left eye. "Do you hear what Bill's saying?"

"Yes—I hear. That infernal mine! Now, it's—sort of—mocking me!"

"Mike, what's come over you? I still don't think you understand. You're mesmerized by that $100,000! Mr. Melikos rescued Liz and Bill—*rescued* them."

Mike shook himself as Potch did sometimes, a great trembling shake that rippled his whole body.

"Yes—I know."

He stepped forward. He held out his hand to Pappa Melikos. "I'm grateful. You saved my kids and Steve. Whatever else you've done—that's all I can remember now. And—God forgive me—at first, I could think only of that hundred thousand! Reckon it *is* time to leave the field when a man feels like that, Melikos. Take my advice—leave the field when dollars set up in front of your eyes and you can't see your kids."

He shook a little. "I've looked into my last shaft, Melikos. I've finished with opal mining. I've finished with—Eldorado."

Melikos stood awkwardly with his right hand on the door handle of his utility. Then he turned and held it out to Mike. "O.K. Everything's O.K. Me—I felt badly about that $100,000, too!" He spread his hands expressively. "But I not give up yet. So long as I can fill the belly and buy gelly I keep on, and my company, we keep on. And we're not doing so badly! Bring grandmother, sister, aunt from Greece. Take *my* advice—you keep on, too."

"Felt badly—about the hundred thousand . . . ?" Mike repeated.

"Yeah. Papadopolous company got that. Back home—in Greece—he and my family enemy. Bad show—don't you think?"

Then he jumped into his vehicle, started the engine and turned the nose down the sharp runway. He didn't look back but rattled away across the flat, back to his own shaft and his inspection of the hole he had been gouging yesterday.

Mike's body shrank and huddled itself together. "So it wasn't him . . ." he said, dazed. "It was that Papadopolous lot—that new lot only here a few weeks—who got the money."

"Mike," May said gently, "you've still got Liz and Bill and Steve. Come and have a cup of tea."

A slow grin spread over Mike's weather-beaten face. "You're great, May," he said. "Reckon you know the worthwhile things, like kids an' Potch an' even that mong Nancy and a cup of tea."

He put his arm around her shoulders and they walked toward the door, the two boys and Liz following.

"Reckon I'll be a truck driver when we get to town," he said. "Good open-air work that'll keep my muscles trim and my weight down. Reckon that's what I've been afraid of, May—getting fat on a soft job in town. We'll go as soon as Liz has finished her exam. Won't wait until the end of the year."

"Then you meant it—that you'd never dig another shaft?" May was incredulous.

"I meant it." Mike was suddenly sober and tired and ashamed. "Even the kids' safety—for a minute—seemed unimportant against all that money. May, when you get like that—like I said—a man's had it."

"It was only because what they were trying to tell you hadn't sunk in," May said, eyes loving, pressing close to him. "No father loves his kids more than you do, Mike."

Mike grinned over his shoulder at his son and daughter. "Too right! And Liz, you'd better get honors in this exam. You never know—you might have to keep me in my old age."

Liz and Bill, Steve and Potch followed Mike and May into the cool dugout where Nancy sprawled dreaming under the table on her belly, her two short back paws stuck out flat behind her and her head on her front paws. It had been too hot to follow the excited humans out into the white sunshine, and she flashed disdain at Potch now as he, too, sought the open space under the table. She didn't move for him, even though he was hot and her back paws got in the way of his sprawl. Potch, she felt, should be kept on the other side of the wire door.

May looked at her two children and Steve. "What a mess you're in! I'll have to fix those cuts and bruises." She turned on her shining tap to fill the kettle. "They'll need hot water."

And now all the noise of clashing human emotions was over, all the bellowing of the gelly and the flying of the shrapnel-like stone was past and Eldorado was past. All that was left was the washing of the cuts, the rubbing of liniment on the bruises and the doing of that exam. Then the packing-up and the going to Grandma Birch's—who didn't like dogs or Aborigines.

17

Nikos Brings Some News

AFTER the washing and the rubbing and the bandaging were done and they had drunk cups of tea, Liz went to her room to find her red-covered textbook on British history for, although her head was not quite ready for study, she wanted the feel of the book in her hands. Steve went to watch Carl cut and polish the last bits of opal they had taken from Eldorado, and Bill went out into the heat with Potch.

Bill went out partly because he found the cool dugout depressing, but really because he wanted to be alone with Potch. Because soon—just as soon as the exam was over—they were to be separated forever. Bill knew it was forever. He had tried hard to find a way out and knew now there was no way. He had to accept things as they were. He would never blame Liz again; it was he who had been selfish, wanting things his own way.

But he couldn't stop being sad, so he went out into the hot sun of this quiet late Sunday afternoon, when so many of the usual noisy vehicles were still. There was still no wind, and the air was lazy, and the desert swallows were flying just above the ground, whirring at the insects.

There was nowhere to go, and he had nothing to do. He sank down in the shade of an empty oil drum and sniffed the slight tang that came from the opening. Diesel oil. He would remember the Opal Town by the smell of the diesel oil and the throbbing of the engines that pulsed always, far into the night.

"Potch." The dog crept close to him, on its belly, pressing into his legs. Bill sighed, a deep crying sigh. "Potch." He put his arms around the dog and clung to him. "What am I going to do without you?"

Tears burned his eyeballs because he tried to hold them back as he clung to Potch. Presently his shoulders shook with the holding back and Potch wriggled so that he could look up and lick his face. The boy and the dog were still then for a long time. Still and quiet, close to each other. But Bill hoped that Potch wouldn't sense the reason for this terrible sadness, these burning unwept tears, wouldn't know, yet, what was going to happen to him. He cried because he had made up his mind to ask Carl to shoot Potch.

This afternoon, before leaving the mine, Nikos had told him how Potch had alerted him to the danger he and Liz were in, how Potch had, in fact, precipitated their rescue —saved them. Because of that, no matter how badly it hurt, he had to do, in return, what was the kindest and best for Potch—and that was not to condemn him to live alone in this inhospitable land, where he would be an outcast from both dogs and men.

Carl was a good shot and it would be a clean instant death, not a lingering one from hunger or thirst.

But Bill just hoped that Potch didn't know of his decision. He couldn't bear for Potch to know. He wouldn't be able to look into those clear brown eyes that never criticized him, never grew angry with him, never did anything but love him. They were looking at him now, steadily, and they were sad.

He stood up suddenly. He couldn't look at that sadness.

As Bill stood up he saw a bike coming across the flat, coming slowly and wobbling rather badly. Whoever was negotiating the gibbers wasn't a good rider, for he fell off once and had to scramble from under the spinning wheels. Evidently he had to wait to collect himself, for it was a minute or two before he stood the machine upright and remounted.

Bill stared for a long time. It was something to do and it kept him from looking at Potch. Presently he realized the rider was Nikos, and it was Bill's bike he was riding. So he was bringing it home to him.

Until this moment he had forgotten about Nikos—forgotten what Nikos had said about not telling his father who had given him the black eye, even forgotten that after finding the fan shell he had blamed Nikos for being involved in stealing the petrol. Now he frowned with uncertainty . . . Perhaps it had not been Nikos's fan shell—yet would there be two such fossils with a chip out in exactly the same place? But Mr. Melikos had had no part in pegging-in Eldorado, so it was most unlikely—no, surely impossible—that Nikos had had anything to do with milking the ute. This meant that as his father had blamed Mr. Melikos, so he had blamed Nikos—for nothing. Like his father, he would have to say he was sorry.

He was glad to be able to say he was sorry. He liked Nikos, liked teaching him to swim in the water hole and to be as free as he was. Yes, he would be glad to apologize for that black eye. But what a smack it must have been for the bruise to have lasted so long! He stood very straight; he need not feel ashamed that judo and karate had brought him low. And after a few more lessons from Nikos he would be able to defend himself in this manner of fighting, too. In the little time that remained before he left for the city, he would get Nikos to perfect him in this art. It would be very useful at that city school—not that it would be the grammar school now—where everyone would be snooty. But not when they found he was an expert judo and karate man.

He moved forward and, with Potch right on his heels, went down the ramp and across the flat to meet Nikos. They met on the bank of the old bulldozer cutting where Nikos had always waited, where he had been waiting that afternoon which seemed such a long time ago now.

Nikos got off the bike and walked the last fifty yards, almost as though he thought he could move faster on his own legs over the stones. He seemed to want to move quickly, to catch up with Bill. They reached that spot where they had fought together, and Potch greeted the Greek boy with a happy wag of the tail and a quick bark.

"I might have scratched it a bit," Nikos said anxiously. "I fell off once—I need more practice."

"You can have a loan of it whenever you like. At least, as long as we're here. We'll be going in a few weeks—soon as Liz has finished her exam."

"Oh . . ." Nikos seemed to be taken aback, though he had known they were going sometime. Then he went on,

"When we were getting ready to go home this afternoon, I asked Pappa if I might ride the bike in. He was glad to let me. He brought the other one in on the ute, but there wasn't room for two."

"Thanks. I'm glad you rode it in."

"Look, there's the scratch—on the handlebar. I'm sorry I did it."

"Don't worry. I've got to thank you for calling your dad and getting us out of the shaft so quickly. Might have been dead by now."

"It was Potch—the way he barked and barked—that told me you were in trouble," said Nikos. "Anyway, Pappa said fumes from twelve charges wouldn't have killed you— even if you'd stayed all the time in the shaft. Only made you pretty sick."

"Well, I'm sorry anyway that I hit you. You see, after finding the fan shell, I thought you'd milked our ute and most likely had something to do with the disappearance of the compressor."

"It would all be the work of Papadopolous—he would remove the compressor to delay you." Nikos sighed. "And no doubt used the time your pappa and Carl were away looking for the compressor to inspect Eldorado, and decided it was worthwhile pegging you in."

"I'll bet that was his cigarette butt," Bill remembered angrily. "He must be a shrewd fellow."

"Yes, indeed—shrewd enough to use my fan shell. He must have found it somewhere—or stolen it—and left it where you'd see it, so that you would blame my pappa for stopping you getting to the mines warden's office in time. And make trouble for my pappa, too. They hate each other. Back home in Greece, the two families are always fighting—mainly because they belong to different political parties. A feud, you'd call it."

Bill knew all about the feuds that were often transferred from Greece to the new country. There had been trouble before, especially when in the case of two such families, one was lucky at finding opal and the other was not.

"This find isn't going to do Papadopolous any good," Nikos went on. "He tricked your dad, now he's—sort of— being tricked. That company's already fighting among themselves over the dividing of the money. The new fellows aren't satisfied with the share they've been given. Pappa has already heard that one of them is going to tell the mines warden who stole the compressor. Reckon you'll get it back any day now, Bill."

"It's too late," Bill said miserably. "We'll never need a compressor again." Then he managed a smile. "Anyway, I'm glad the trouble between you and me has been cleared up, and thank you for bringing the bike back."

"Bill—you might need the compressor!"

Nikos rested the bike carefully on the ground and licked his lips. Bill saw then that he was trembling a little, that the commonplace tone of their conversation had been hard to endure, that he was bursting with the information he had to impart.

Bill looked at him expectantly.

Nikos's dark eyes were shining now. "Bill, I went down there after you'd gone—when it was safe enough to go down—when the fumes had cleared."

"Down Eldorado—alone . . . ?"

"Yes. Rigas had gone off again with Manolis. I knew he wouldn't be back, for he had tools to sharpen. I got a long rope, tied it to our own hoist and went dov

monkey, like my father did. I had to see what you had
blown out."

Bill was staring.

"You're not angry, Bill? I know I shouldn't have—that
it's your claim. But somehow I had to know whether your
work—and getting nearly killed—had been worthwhile."

"Yes—and has it?" Bill was steely quiet now, but his
hand sought the soft hair of Potch's head, felt the warmth
of it and the trust.

"I think it has. The blast has uncovered a trace, Bill—a
very good one. I saw all the colors of fire, all the colors of
the sea, all the colors of the sky, down there. It could be
good, Bill."

Bill stood very still, immobilized by the news. His father
had said that he was finished with Eldorado—that never
again would he look down another shaft. He had told Mr.
Melikos that he was finished with Eldorado.

"Your pappa—does he know this?"

"No-o. I didn't tell him."

That was when Nikos began to shake again, and Bill understood why. This was something Mr. Melikos would be
very angry about, not because Nikos had gone down another mine but because he did not tell his father what he
saw there. No Greek boy could be more disobedient than
this. Now Bill understood how much freedom he had
taught Nikos.

"I wanted you to know first—it's your mine. But the
way your father left yesterday—I had a feeling you might
never go back to it. And we Greeks believe that it is bad
luck, very bad luck, not to finish out a shaft completely.
But please, Bill, don't tell my pappa—don't let him know
that I told you first."

"Of course not. Indeed I wouldn't."

"He would be so angry."

"I know, and I'll never tell him. But now I must go home. I didn't tell Mum I was coming out. Tomorrow I'll see you at the mine. Come on, Potch, you need a drink." He smiled at Nikos, trying to make up for the Greek boy's obvious disappointment at this quick finish to their meeting. "Thanks very much for bringing the bike—and the news. We'd have been out there in the morning, anyway. You're a great mate, Nikos."

As he thrust his left foot onto the left pedal and swung his right leg over the seat, Bill hoped that he hadn't told a lie about being at the mine tomorrow. After all, his father had said he was finished.

He whistled to Potch and set off toward Watson's dugout while Nikos turned a little to the left to his own hill.

Bill rode with great aplomb, knowing that there was no better bike rider in the Opal Town. But he made no indecent haste. He didn't want Nikos to know at this stage that he had changed the color of Bill's sky from gray to rose, or raised such wild excitement in his breast, or given life back to Potch.

18

❖

Off Again—
On Again

ONCE out of sight of Nikos, Bill rode his bike fiercely, and though he had to get off at the bottom of the ramp, he ran his machine up the slope, dropped it at the fly-wire door, leaving the wheels still spinning, and thumped inside.

"Dad—Dad—the monkey! It's worked! There's opal down there—Nikos says so!"

May came from the kitchen where she had been preparing the roast of beef that she had decided now would bolster drooping spirits at the evening meal, and Mike came from his workroom where he had already started to sort the specimen collection of eight years for removal to the city or for sale, and Liz came from the depths of a chapter on the Renaissance.

"If you're having a joke!" threatened May.

"What are you yelling about?" growled Mike.

Liz just looked and waited to hear more.

Bill repeated then what Nikos had told him.

"If this is true, Bill," his father said quietly, "the seam—

190

after the pocket in the north claim—must have doubled back and downward. It does happen—as you yourself tried to remind me."

He gave a deep sigh. He was afraid to believe his son's news, but he realized that he must at least take one more look down a shaft. And if this story was true he must look at once, before Melikos acted on the assumption that he had written off Eldorado for good and felt at liberty to make his own plans for taking it over. That he would be planning to do this was certain. How many times had a mine—abandoned in bitter disappointment by one man— proved a treasure house for the next?

So if there was any truth in this story there was no time to waste.

Bill was sent hurrying for Steve and Carl, and Mike began to reload the utility with all the gear brought in yesterday. The winch, the motor, the ropes, the buckets, the picks and shovels, the series of ladders. As the days were still lengthening toward summer and it would be daylight until nearly seven o'clock, there would be time to set up gear for an early working start on the morrow—that is, if the story was true.

Carl was soon helping with the loading, though grunting now and again. Such on-and-off tactics were against his sense of order and precision, and he didn't refrain from saying, as he had said earlier, that Mike had been too hasty in removing the gear in the first place. But he didn't labor the point. Carl had learned long ago that emotions must never distort a man's clear vision of what he had to do. And he saw clearly now that they must return to the mine as quickly as possible.

May and Liz were left with the roast beef, the men

promising to be back to eat it as soon as darkness fell. For Liz and her mother, there was no question of going out to the mine. With Carl back at work—even if his backbone was still creaking—there was no need for them, not even for Liz. Neither did Liz want to go; like her father, she was frightened to believe the story.

The few men who had been working on the field earlier in the day had finished by the time they arrived. With the approach of the utility one or two came from their shacks or tents to see who was arriving, and shrugged and passed some remark about this "off again-on again" Watson "company." But no one was really surprised. Rigas had told the story of the rescue drama, and those who knew thought it natural that Mike should want to see what the monkey had revealed, if anything.

The broken windlass—the sight of which made Mike shudder—was quickly tossed aside for the motorized winch, and the rest of their gear, still inadequate without the compressor, was set back in place.

With Bill on the winch, Mike went down on the first bucket, then Carl, then Steve. Bill followed on the re-erected ladders.

Daylight had faded sufficiently now for it to be dark at the bottom of the shaft, but the long flex from the generator gave them light. The twelve charges had blown two good-sized holes and Mike began at once to pick gently, with almost trembling fingers, in a corner of the hole farthest in.

"It's here all right," he said with awe. "Look at this seam—thin as a wafer, but sparkling with every color of the rainbow. Gem opal! It's a narrow lead, but I've never seen a better one. And there's the slide—clear as a map.

Look, it goes this way. Twelve feet in front of that slide, Carl, and we'll find a fortune!"

Carl smiled slowly. "We've a lot of rock to move before we can be sure, but you could be right."

"We'll start at daylight in the morning!"

"Dad . . ." Bill was hesitant but hopeful, "may Steve and I work with you tomorrow?"

"Monday? Work with us on Monday? What about school?"

"Please . . ."

"Let them, Mike," Carl said, sucking hard on his pipe and hollowing in his cheeks as he sucked. "They're the reason we're back here at this moment."

"All right. You're in it—the pair of you. In fact, we'll be glad of your help. I've a mind to see that rock moved fast. But you'll have to be up before daylight."

"And now," sniffed Carl, "I can smell May's roast beef from here. Steve and I are going to invite ourselves to this Sunday's tea, Mike."

The next day they didn't have to move twelve feet of rock to get to the front of Mike's slide. Before midday they had cleared the shaft of the already blasted rock and were following the lead. Even Bill and Steve were each wielding a small two-headed pick, working gently and methodically, as experienced miners wield a pick, for they were working under the sharp eyes and tongues of the partners.

It was Bill's pick that revealed the fortune.

Like the others, he was gouging beneath the seam-line, starting a foot or so beneath the trace and working carefully upward until the ceiling of his hole was this lead— narrow in width at first and then suddenly leaping and bulging into a pocket. And there it was—the most glorious parcel of fiery opal that man could wish to see. Opal to light a world.

He said, voice aquiver, "Dad—I've found it—the bit with my name on it!"

It was a chunk of opal, alive and blazing with red fire, alive with a million spirits of tossing color. There was blue, purple, Irish green and, above all, there was red. Sometimes it was the yellow-red of fire, sometimes the magenta tone of crushed strawberries. Whatever the color, it darted, tossed, flared, swirled in a surge of movement like a living thing. *Living!* That was the word.

No wonder, after that first gasp, they stood silently. Just looking—feasting on a beauty not surpassed anywhere by any other single element, or so capable of demonstration in the confined space of even the smallest stone.

"I've never seen better!" Mike breathed the words, as though he feared to disturb a loveliness that had taken millions of years to form and had lain undisturbed for millions of years more. Was that why the colors were dancing now—dancing because at last perfection was to be revealed, no longer to be weighed down and imprisoned by the weight of unresponsive sandstone but lifted to the warmth of the sun and the joy and admiration of a million eyes?

For minutes, Carl's pipe had struck out from his mouth like a dead stick, no whiff of smoke from the bowl, no movement of the stem. Now he took it from his mouth and bent closer to look at the opal.

"A fortune . . ."

"They got $100,000 in the north claim," Mike said. "I reckon there's $200,000 here."

"Ja."

They gouged then without thought of time. But they gouged gently and carefully, and wrapped their fortune in the calico bags Carl never failed to carry. By the time they were satisfied to go home to tell May and Liz and to share cold roast beef and tomato and lettuce, the sky was a jet-black ceiling studded with the sparkling white rivets of stars.

19

Carl and
the Future

For a man who had just helped to uncover a fortune from the earth, Carl was surprisingly quiet during that evening meal. And when it was finished he sat chewing hard on the stem of his pipe, appearing sometimes to be about to swallow the whole thing, bowl as well.

At first his quietness was hardly noticed. May and Liz, Bill and Steve and Mike were making noise enough. Even Potch, aware that something extraordinary and exciting—something good—had happened, added his quota by growling at Nancy each time she edged in between him and Bill. This was so unusual and ungentlemanly that Nancy retreated to the space under the sideboard, looking out at Potch with disillusioned eyes.

"We can settle now for that house at Glenelg," May said, moving between table and sink with dirty dishes. "At least there's no doubt about it this time, and we can make up our minds." She glanced with happy eyes toward the parcel of opal, still sandstone encrusted, that sat in the center of her sideboard. "And Glenelg won't be too far from Grandma Birch at Mitcham."

"But far enough for Potch to be safe—and Steve." Bill beamed.

"And Kathy," said Liz.

"Of course, and Kathy." May smiled. "Two of you to dress up, Liz—I'll like that."

That was when Carl took his pipe from his mouth. "I've been thinking . . ."

"I knew something was going on," May said, "sitting there, sucking that thing, saying nothing—not even that the salad was tasty or the meat tender. Don't reckon you knew what you were eating."

"Don't reckon . . ." Carl agreed humbly.

"Well, come on, out with it, what *have* you been thinking?"

"I've been thinking that—if Steve will let me—I'd like to adopt him."

There was silence for a moment while all eyes looked toward Carl.

"It isn't something that has just come to mind," he said mildly. "I've thought about it many times. But I've also realized that if I was going to return to my own country, it wouldn't be right to adopt him."

"And aren't you going to return?" Mike asked.

"Yes—but not to stay. Not after finding all that opal. It wouldn't be fair just to take it and go."

"But you were going back," May reminded him. "You've been saying that if we didn't find opal, you would leave the opal fields when we left."

"Yes—that's what I intended to do. I intended to go home and try to pick up life there again. But now—this find—" and he waved an arm to the play of lights on the sideboard, "has changed all that. When a man digs up a fortune from the earth of a country, I feel that country is entitled to his services."

"But your own country—Austria?"

"I shall always love Austria," Carl said simply. "It is my birthplace, and a man never ceases to love his birthplace." He smiled across the table to Steve. "It's the same, or more so, with the Aborigine to whom his birthplace—his country—is almost his religion, isn't it, Steve?"

"What about your mother?" May said.

"I'll go home and see my mother, and make sure she wants for nothing for the rest of her life, then I'll come back." Again he looked at Steve. "But before I go, I'd like to see that adoption made legal. What about it, Steve?"

The boy had been sitting very still, his face expressionless, while the talk bandied about him. Now he smiled, and it was like the lighting up of a great lamp as eyes, teeth and skin suddenly sparkled and his face came alive.

"Yes," he said, "I'd like that." And the smile became a grin. "So long as I can still be a policeman."

Carl nodded. "Yes—that mustn't be changed. I think, as a member of the Force, you can do a lot for your people. But I won't take you to Europe with me. Not this time, anyway. Later on, when you're a few years older, will be the time. But perhaps, while I'm away, May and Mike will look after you."

"We will indeed," said May. "That house is going to have five bedrooms at least, maybe six."

Steve's face had sobered and he looked toward Carl. "When you come back, what will you do? Where will you settle?"

Carl smiled. "I'll come back to the Opal Town—and you with me. Maybe I'll build a new motel for tourists—maybe I'll just try my luck again. I like it here in the heat and the sun and the color. I'll stay here for as long as you need me, Steve."

The boy relaxed then. He didn't know anything about being a front-line soldier or a spearhead, but he did know that with Carl beside him the way ahead would be sure and direct.

"I've been doing some thinking, too—sort of planning," said Mike, "and the more I listen to May's description of the house at Glenelg and other ideas for the future, the more I realize I'll have to put those plans into action."

"You said Eldorado would be your last shaft," May bristled.

"It will, I promise you. But you know opal is in my blood—that I can't divorce myself from it."

"What are you getting at?" May was frowning with suspicion.

"I'm going to turn opal buyer."

May stood with her hands on her hips, looking at him.

"Listen, we will have to invest the money we get from the sale of the parcel. That will be our capital. Apart from buying the house and the new furniture and a new car—things we really need—we can't live on our capital. If we did, it would only last a very short time, especially the way you're talking of spending it! So we have to make it earn money. What better way—as far as I am concerned, at least—than by using it to buy and sell opal?"

May wasn't very good at the economics of living or not living off one's capital, so she waited to hear more, at the same time keeping an eye on Carl whose business sense she valued. He was nodding his head.

"And May—I'll still be handling this precious stone, still close to it."

"He'll be a good buyer," Carl said. "He knows opal—best classer on the field. He won't make too many mistakes. There won't be many 'cracky' parcels fobbed off on him."

"That's it," Mike agreed easily. "I know my opal. Of course, I'll make a mistake now and again—all buyers do."

"Not you!" said May, suddenly confident and enthusiastic and beginning to smile with some wickedness. "You know what it means, don't you?" she quizzed. "You'll have to wear a spotless white shirt, good pants and a tie all the time, just like that immaculate Japanese buyer. And what's more, you'll have to wear your teeth. No opal buyer is ever seen without teeth."

Mike's face fell. "I hadn't thought of that."

Liz and May were laughing together. "We were wondering," May said, "how we were going to get you to the stage of wearing those teeth all the time. After all, in the city—in Glenelg—people don't go around without their teeth."

20

The End of
the Year

IT WAS May, surprisingly enough, who brought the family back to the practical aspects of living. There were many unfinished tasks to complete, she said, before their move from the Opal Town, which would be timed for immediately after the school break-up and Speech Night.

Eldorado had to be worked out completely. As Nikos said, it was bad luck not to do so. Liz had to complete her studies and pass the exam, for this was her way and path in life, and Bill had to try to pass his end-of-the-year exams, too, so that he would not go backward when he started at the grammar school. After all, if he wanted to remain close to the mining he loved, what better could he do than get some education and become a mining engineer?

That was when Carl again took the pipe from his mouth and said, with something of a sigh, "This town is going to alter, Bill, as it has over the last eight years. It's forsaken the old manual methods for that of machinery—the hand-driven windlass for the motorized winch, carbide lamps for electricity—and doubled its permanent population. It will go on altering, faster and faster, becoming less and less a frontier town. It will probably also go on being the largest opal field in the world, producing the world's finest opal. But modern living will take the sting out of our summer sun of 120 degrees, and a good north-south road will rob 'outback' of its meaning."

Mike came in then. "What Carl says is true, Bill. By the time you're a man, living here won't be very much different from living in more ordinary places. I think you'll come back to opal, but by then it'll probably be a specialist's game. In any case, even if it isn't, if you qualify as a mining engineer you'll have a trade to fall back on when the time comes—as it has for me—for you to give up being just an opal miner."

Bill listened to these words of wisdom and was satisfied to return to school in the morning. After all, he had found the piece with his name on it, Potch would live to be old in comfort and Steve would always have Carl. He even surprised Mr. Robbins by doing some extraordinarily neat geometrical and trigonometrical drawings.

Liz was happy, too, to go to school that next morning, with light feet and no feeling of guilt because she loved learning. And in the afternoon she went to the hospital. Again she found Kathy and Ruthie on the cool passage floor, playing with the red ball amidst squeals of laughter from the baby.

Liz told Kathy the news of their good fortune quietly, knowing that material wealth was not much understood by her friend, but she did expect part of her news to stir the dark girl.

"I'll still be leaving, Kathy," she said quietly, "but you

can come and live with us in the town. We'll live in a proper house, something like this hospital, with a bath—perhaps a pink one—and beds and sheets, just like you have here. You can go to school with me, and wear pretty dresses."

Kathy listened just as quietly as she let Ruthie climb onto her lap and pull her hair and try to look in her ear, but she didn't say anything.

"Our house will be near the sea," Liz said, "and you'll be able to swim, like we did in the water hole. But there'll be lots more water—blue water—and waves. And there'll be a town—much bigger than the Opal Town—with trams and trains and many more people."

"I don't know trams an' trains . . ." Kathy said.

"You'll soon learn," Liz said. "It'll be exciting."

Kathy turned her head to look into Liz's face. "But Sister's teaching me to make custard, Liz—an' *you* can't make custard. An' who'd mind Ruthie? An' . . ." The dark eyes glowed. "The other sister—Sister Alice—is going to town, too, for a long holiday, and Sister Joan says I can stay here, an' help her, an' learn to be a—what d'ye call it? —an aide, a nursing aide."

"Oh . . ." Liz felt deflated.

"I can't be proper nurse, Liz—not for years, maybe never, because I have to pass exams, like you. And I haven't had enough school—though I'm going back to-morrow so I know the songs for break-up. Liz, Sister Joan says I've got soft fingers for aide."

"That's wonderful, Kathy," Liz said. "You have got soft fingers and a soft heart, and you're kind. You'll be a wonderful nursing aide."

"I'll teach Margaret, too. Reckon she'll want to learn

from me when she sees what I can do—Sister Joan says so."

"Yes—I'm sure she will."

"An' when Steve's a copper," Kathy went on confidentially, "he'll marry me."

Liz sat back on her haunches. "Has . . . has he asked you yet?" This, she felt, was getting away to a very early start.

"No—but he told me to learn to make custard, didn't he?"

"Yes."

"Well—that's it." Kathy was very certain. "An' I'm going to learn to sew, and make a new romper thing for Ruthie."

Sister Joan came from the kitchen then. She was smiling. "Don't look so floored, Liz," she laughed, "and when you leave the Opal Town, remember, your kindness and your understanding were the foundation for the making of that custard. Or this spearhead—if you can see what I mean."

Liz snatched Ruthie from Kathy then, and squeezed the baby hard and kissed her, because she would have astonished and embarrassed Kathy if she had attacked her in this way, which was what she wanted to do, and also because she wanted to hide the tears she couldn't hold back. Then she thrust the child back into Kathy's arms and ran down the passage and out into the strong sunlight.

The weeks to the school break-up and Speech Night, held in the community hall, were busy for everyone, and the events came very quickly. It was a hot night with no moon. The town was black, except where a light globe at the entrance to a dugout beamed like an earth-star or the pale glow from the dusty windows of the two stores and the gash of light from the hall lit the gibbers.

As it was nearly mid-December, many of the miners without families had already gone south, leaving only the few hardy permanent residents and the families who were waiting until school finished. For the next couple of months, while summer heat raged, the Opal Town would be a ghost town.

Nevertheless, the hall was crowded. Even those remaining adults who didn't have children at the school were present because it was a social event. Some dogs barked outside while those who had owners came in when they could get past the doorkeeper and sought their masters in a sea of unfamiliar dark-clad legs. Potch, being large, had to crawl under the wooden chairs on his belly.

All the men present wore white shirts and ties with the trousers of their best suits, and the women, still much in the minority, wore their gayest and best dresses, making splashes of color, like opal, against the unlined walls and spider webs in the high beam of the roof. Once a woman screamed when a scorpion scuttled under her chair and everyone moved in the chase.

May wore the pale blue silk dress which she kept for special occasions, and had had her hair in rollers all day so that it stood up in a semblance of the style that a city hairdresser would give her.

Mike's hair had been dried out by the sun and wouldn't lie down despite a thorough plastering with hair oil. He was uncomfortable in his white shirt, tie, trousers, leather shoes that pinched and his teeth. He sighed to think that these were the screws he always would have to endure as an opal buyer.

The schoolchildren were grouped in a body on forms in the front, but there was no dais, just a wooden table with a large photograph of Queen Elizabeth II hanging on the wall behind it. They sang the songs they had been practicing all the year, including "Waltzing Matilda" and "Song of Australia," and then there was the prize-giving, which included a First for Steve and a Much Improved for Kathy but nothing for Bill, who just hadn't been able to make up for a year's lack of interest.

Then came the announcement that Liz, the only senior pupil, had passed her exams with honors. Mike forgot how hot and uncomfortable his clothes were, and May thanked Mr. Robbins in her special voice.

Surprisingly, among those present were Mr. Melikos and Nikos, who were planning to stay on in the heat until they had worked out their claim. Pappa Melikos moved to congratulate Mike on his daughter's good results.

"Next year . . ." and his laugh boomed and his thick black brows twitched, "perhaps someone congratulate me. My Nikos, he an Australian Greek—got very cheeky." He bent forward, confidentially. "Do you know, Mike Watson, he has persuaded me—his pappa—that he must have the more school next year. And so I agree. This Mr. Robbins-teacher, nice man—knows all about shells and many things."

Then Pappa Melikos moved toward the door because he was very hot and Nikos followed obediently behind, smiling broadly. Bill was several seats away but Nikos took a petrified fan shell from his pocket and flashed it at him. They both understood. It *was* a lucky shell for Nikos.

With the business of the night over, the noise rose as people moved and rasped their chairs. The dogs barked louder than ever and ran in and out at will, frightening Potch into immobility under Bill's seat.

Liz, Kathy, Steve and Bill had been sitting together on the same backless form. Now they stood up and moved into the crowd of parents, Potch's hot body keeping close to their legs. For all of them there was still some unreality about the events of the last few weeks, some unreality in the partings that were soon to take place.

Kathy was taller than Liz and now she whispered in her friend's ear, "Ruthie walked today, Liz. Took four proper steps. Tomorrow, Sister Joan says, she will do twice that."

"You must write every week and tell me how she is doing," Liz said, and was grateful to know that that house in Glenelg would have many bedrooms. There would be no permanent partings.

Author's Note

OPAL is Australia's national gemstone. It is also the world's most brilliantly colored precious stone. It may contain not only all the basic colors of the spectrum—red, orange, yellow, indigo, green, violet—but all the in-between shades as well. These colors flash and flare like fire, making the stone seem alive.

Mineral common opal—which has no lights or "fire"—is found in quantity in many parts of the world and can be of various colors, such as blue, white, amber. It is mostly opaque like china and is practically worthless. In Australia, common opal is known as "potch." But top-quality precious opal is more rare than the diamond, and consequently more valuable.

Australia produces 95 per cent of the world's precious opal; the other 5 per cent is mined at Querétaro in Mexico and Rainbow Ridge in Nevada.

Scientists believe that opal began—perhaps 100 million years ago—as a liquid with the consistency of a thin jelly.

The liquid was a solution of silica, or pure sand, dissolved in water by high temperature and pressure or the action of certain chemicals in the water. This jellylike material seeped into holes and cracks beneath the earth's surface. As it dried out and solidified it became the mineral known as opal—most of it common opal, but some of it the rare and precious gem material.

Not very long ago, two Australian scientists discovered the reason for the difference between dull common opal and the sparkling gem opal. An electron microscope revealed that opal is composed of an infinite number of tiny balls of silica, measured in millionths of an inch.

If these balls have settled in orderly fashion—the way marbles will do if shaken down into a box—then spaces are left where the curves of the balls do not touch. Light passing through these cracks is diffracted, or bent, producing the flashing colors of a gem opal. The more perfect the settling of the tiny balls of silica, the more brilliant the color. But in common opal the spheres have settled unevenly and light cannot get through. It is like a window with the blind drawn. Sometimes in a piece of potch there will be one tiny spot from which will come a flash of fire.

The less water in opal, the more durable the stone. The Australian stone is of such high quality, particularly good for fashioning into jewelry, because the inland areas of the country, where opal is found, are among the world's driest. Australia's biggest opal field, Coober Pedy (an Aboriginal term meaning "white fellows' burrows"), has an average annual rainfall of only five inches. And even that is erratic. The five inches may all fall in one big "rain," or there may be three years between rains.

There is no easy way to find opal. "Floaters" are the

only surface indication of its presence. These are bits of bleached or crazed (cracked) opal freed by centuries of weathering from the sides of gullies or creeks. Since floaters are always washed downhill, the man who finds them follows the trail uphill, searching for more evidence. At what seems to be the beginning of the trail he starts to dig. All of the major Australian opal fields were found by accident, mostly by stockmen riding after cattle, or sometimes by a prospector looking for gold. On a proved opal field, men simply try their luck by sinking shaft after shaft, often without reward.

In the early days on the opal fields, a miner might find opal near the surface, but the shallow grounds have all been worked out now, and a shaft may go down a hundred feet. Before the invention of the motorized winch, compressor and power plant, men had to rely on their own muscles to dig holes and clear out the rubble, using greenhide buckets and mulga logs as windlasses. The miners' main aid then was gelignite, and it still is. They have to be careful to count the shots, or "fractures," when the explosive is set off, for an unexploded charge is a danger.

As the miner sinks his hole he watches continually for good "trace" or a "lead" (common opal, sometimes with some color in it) and a "slide." A slide is a small fault in the earth's crust, and opal is often found in front of it, the movement having created a crack or an empty space in which the opal "jelly" could lodge and solidify.

When a miner finds opal, whether in a continuing seam or in separate cavities, it is generally in relatively small pieces which fit together like a jigsaw puzzle. The miner gouges the pieces very gently out of their sandstone bed with a small two-headed miner's pick.

If a good "parcel," or find, of opal has been made in an

area, then the shafts, or claims, are often very close together. A Miner's Right allows a miner to stake a claim to
a specified plot of ground 150 feet square. He is entitled to
claim all the opal he finds beneath the surface within the
boundaries of that 150 square feet.

But if he overlooks some good stones in the mullock, or
refuse, he hoists to the surface and discards, he can't protest if someone else finds them while "noodling" his
dump. To noodle is to sift through the mullock with an
iron bar or a small pick, looking for gems the owner of the
claim might have missed. As there is little work on an opal
field for anyone except miners, many Aborigines make
their living this way.

Aborigines are the race of dark-skinned people who in-
habited Australia before the coming of the white man, and
they still live within all the areas where opal is found. An-
thropologists believe that Aborigines first came to Australia from the north about twenty thousand years ago, when
stepping stones of islands stretched between Asia and Australia and the longest stretch of water to be crossed in
primitive crafts was only about eighty miles. Although it
seems logical to assume that the Aborigines came from
Asia, it has been proved that they are of the same blood
group as Europeans.

Apart from their dog, the dingo, the Aborigines did not
bring animals with them, nor seeds, and Australia at that
time had no plants that could be cultivated as crops, such
as wheat, or any animals that could be domesticated or
herded, such as horses or sheep. It was the white man, who
nearly died of starvation in his first years of colonization,
who brought all the seeds and fruit trees and sheep and
cattle and horses that flourish in Australia today.

When European settlement began in 1788, there were about three hundred thousand Aborigines, divided into five hundred tribes, scattered throughout Australia, including the dry inland areas. Each tribe occupied its own "country" and stayed within its boundaries. The tribes were not warlike, and one never tried to seize another's territory even if the land was better.

They did not wear clothes, because there was no fiber that could be made into cloth, and they did not live in permanent houses because they had to move from place to place—"go walkabout"—in search of food. In a land that only offered such food as grasses and roots, kangaroos and emus, snakes, iguanas and, on the coast, fish, a man had to spend his time hunting and food-gathering just to live. Wherever he happened to be, he would build a temporary shelter of bark or bush which he would leave behind when he moved on.

The Aborigines still lived much as they had thousands of years ago, and the white settlers looked down on them because of their primitive way of life. But the settlers did not appreciate the skills that the Aborigines had developed in order to survive in this difficult land, nor did they understand the complex life and law of the tribes.

Although there were no chieftains as such, the tribal elders were obeyed. Every member of the tribe had his place and was looked after from birth to death. Each tribe was a separate group, living in its own territory and speaking its own dialect, but throughout the country customs were similar, especially in regard to the land and the sacredness of boundaries.

An Aborigine's whole life was tied to his particular territory. It was where he was born and lived, where his ancestors had walked since the "Dreamtime," the very beginning of time, and where all the places sacred to him were located. He never crossed over the boundaries into another tribe's country except by invitation, perhaps to join in a friendly corroboree or dance. For to enter another's territory without permission was to invite death.

This was one of the reasons why the coming of the Europeans so demoralized the Aborigines. When an Aborigine was pushed out of his bit of country, he had nowhere to go. He couldn't retreat or fall back into the next tribe's territory, because that meant death, too.

On the green fringes of the east coast and in Tasmania, most of the tribes were wiped out in the early years of white settlement. In the north and the more remote areas of the country, however, they survived and are now on the increase.

For many years white Australians believed that the Aborigines were a dying race and that the best that could be done for them was to give them handouts of food and clothing. Over the last few years this attitude has changed and now attempts are being made to give them equal education and opportunity. But so many years have been lost that it may take several generations before the Aborigine can find his rightful place in modern Australian society.

Glossary

❖

bindy-eye—the very prickly burr of a low-growing creeping plant

bore—a windmill-powered pump that brings water to the surface from natural underground storages; sometimes the water is saline, sometimes fresh

dink—give a ride to someone on a bicycle

dog-man—a construction worker whose job is to guide girders into position in a building's structure

Dreamtime—to the Aborigines, the very beginning of time

fractures—explosive charges

galah—a beautiful Australian parrot, but a derogatory term when used to describe a person

gibbers—the small stones that lie over thousands of miles of the dry inland area of Australia

go walkabout—move around the country; wander

gunya—a shelter made of boughs

humpies—rough, impermanent shelters made by the Aborigines

kungka—woman
louse the dumps—same as noodle
mob—as used here, another word for tribe or group
mong—a mongrel, sometimes used as a derogatory term
    for a person
mulga—a stunted tree with needlelike foliage
mullock—mining refuse; rubble
new chums—men new to opal mining; novices
nong—a derogatory term meaning a fool
noodle—search the rubble from a mine for bits of opal
nyitayira—man
pegged—the 150 square feet of ground allowed for an opal
    claim is marked out by a peg and arms of stones at
    right angles at each corner
potch—mineral common opal, a practically worthless
    stone lacking the "fire" of precious opal
sump—the bottom portion of an engine
tucker-bag—a container for carrying food
tucker money—money to pay for food
wag it—be absent from school without leave
willy-willy—a vertical spiral of red dust
zac—a slang term for a sixpence